I0672974

I Am What They Made Me

Ilon Francis

1

Winter in New York can be brutal. The freezing temps and the winds that feel like they're trying to rip your skin off. The dirty piles of snow that last until April. But it can also be exquisite. This is what Misty was thinking as she sipped her drink and watched the snow falling in the glow of the streetlights. Her date was rambling on about something. This guy was chatty!! She giggled, hoping it was the right response, but knowing it didn't really matter. He wanted her so he wouldn't say anything if it wasn't. Next came a blonde joke. Another one. Misty was blonde tonight with green eyes. "Tres exotic!" she thought and giggled again. Her date was Paul. They'd met earlier that evening in Whole Foods. He'd helped her pick the perfect avocado, asked her out, and here they were. What Paul didn't know was that she had been watching him for weeks. Misty had watched him and learned his patterns. She'd even spoken to him once, but he didn't remember her. Misty had long red unruly curls that day. Paul was one of four men that Misty needed to find, but he was the first that she'd had any contact with. Everything was going according to plan. Misty was just flirty enough, just aloof enough to keep him hooked. Misty needed him to take her back to his place. That's when things would get interesting.

Do you dream in color? Misty did. She hadn't thought too much about until she heard "Better Man" by Pearl Jam. Some say dreams hold the answers to your heart's deepest desire. While others say dreams expose your deepest fears. Some people use their dreams to decide which lottery numbers to play. Misty just thought they were great little movies that played in your head. She'd never gotten any great revelation from any of them. They were mostly lighthearted. She didn't remember most of them, but she knew how she felt when she woke up. The creepy ones always left a little residue. Like the one where you can't move. Misty hated those. Those are supposed to mean that you don't feel you're in control of your life. If that's true, kids should have them every night. Especially foster kids. Maybe they do, but their minds don't hold on to that part, they just move past it to the running and jumping and monster dreams. Misty guessed the deepest fears part could be true too. Like if you have a secret, you desperately want to keep from coming out, but you feel it creeping closer and closer to the surface. Rising through the muck like a body that was weighed down with cinder blocks but somehow slipped loose and washed ashore.

Last night's dream was one of the creepy ones. Misty was floating. Floating in a sea surrounded by whales. They were humming and swimming around her like a dance. The water was warm, and she liked the salty taste. The humming got more rhythmic, and Misty hummed along. One whale came up to her looking at her with one giant eye and she heard it speak. It was speaking to her telepathically. It said "You know the way and you know what to do. The path has been laid out for you. You are the only one who knows the truth and only you can…" a giant wave forced the whale under water and sent Misty deep into the depths of the sea. As Misty was trying to swim to the surface, she noticed that she wasn't in a sea of water. It was blood. Misty didn't panic, though. Somehow, that was better. Misty still had to get to the surface. She swam hard and harder, but it seemed like she wasn't getting anywhere. When Misty couldn't hold her breath any longer she gave in. The warm salty blood flowed into her lungs like it was air. "Can I breathe blood?" Misty wondered. Then the convulsions began but Misty still didn't panic. They felt like dance moves. "I'm going to drown in a sea of blood dancing with singing whales.

Misty awoke with a start, breathing hard and sweating. She felt like she had been holding her breath. She sucked in all the air she could. Misty had woken up like this more and more often lately, but she couldn't remember the dream. Misty tried going back to sleep to see if it would come back, but it never did. She knew it was a bad one, though. They always left her with that feeling. Misty went into the bathroom and splashed water on her face. Misty knew what was causing the dreams. It was the plan, but she didn't know if the dreams were warning her not to go forward or pushing her forward. "Oh, well," she thought and went back to bed.

Ryan was running. Running and crying. The branches slapped him in the face. He could feel something running down his cheeks, but he didn't know if it was sweat, tears or blood. All he knew was that he had to get away from here. His feet were heavy, and he couldn't see through the tears, but he kept running. It wasn't supposed to be like this. It was supposed to be a prank. They said they just wanted to scare her and get a good laugh. That was it. He liked her. She was pretty and smart. Not like the other kids from the foster home. They talked about going to college and living in the city afterward. His friends said he was nuts, though. He couldn't have a girlfriend from the foster home. So, he agreed to play the prank on her. Things went so bad, as bad as bad could get and that was still the understatement of the century. There was so much blood. He could still hear her screaming, asking for his help. But all he could do was run away.

"No! No!" he cried as he sat up in his bed. He looked around. The room was empty. It was always empty. How long could he live like this? Forever, he guessed. He deserved to be miserable for what he'd done. If only he could make it right.

He knew that was impossible. He didn't know where she was. He had been trying to track her down for years. Maybe he could apologize. "Ha." He laughed out loud. "How would that apology go? Hello, I'm Ryan, do you remember me. I'm one of the guys that attacked you. I'm sorry." He said to the empty room. Maybe, maybe, maybe. He didn't even know if she was still alive.

That night, the police had come to their homes. They'd come up with a story when they went to Paul's house to clean up. His basement was their meeting place. It had a separate entrance, so his parents never saw them come and go. They had told their parents that they were all together and had no clue what had happened and didn't have anything to do with it. That was enough for the cops. They weren't even asked to come in for a lineup. They went on with life as usual, the way only kids can. School was all a buzz about it a few days later and they listened like they were hearing it for the first time. Paul added to the story, claiming he heard she was a prostitute. That took off faster than the space shuttle. He even heard teachers repeating it. She never came back to school. They heard she'd run away. He couldn't say he blamed her. But they heard no official story. She was gone, and he had to live with what he'd done.

His friends went on like nothing happened, but he couldn't. He gradually stopped hanging with them and was relieved when they stopped calling. He had always been a happy, outgoing kid, but that all changed that night. He barely went out after that night. His parents thought it was the trauma of having someone his age disappear, but eventually chalked it up to hormones. He went on to college and law school. He never saw those guys again, but he heard bits and pieces of their lives from his parents. He was an attorney now. He represented and mentored troubled youth. His major lesson was how one mistake can change your whole life and that good judgement was your best weapon. He looked at the clock. It was 4am. He had a long day today. He and his friend Troy coached a basketball team. The team was a group of kids from various group homes. It was a part of his mentoring program.

Across town Goldie awoke similarly. "No more! No more!!" She screamed in the darkness. She had dreamed that she was a stallion and was being forced to mate with every mare on the farm. There were a lot of mares. "Are you okay?!" Misty screamed as she came running into the room. "I'm okay just a bad dream". Goldie said. "No more candy before bed for you" Misty joked. Goldie laid back down panting. She knew why she had the bad dream. She mentored LGBTQ+ youth and one of their stories really got to her. A young man who was raised by devout Christians who thought that conversion treatment would "fix" him. The mix of horror and sadness in his eyes was haunting. Goldie was a trans woman, so she knew how cruel people could be. Blessedly, she hadn't experienced it at home. Her mom was a flower child that believed in aliens, healing crystals, spirits and just about everything else people told her couldn't exist. Goldie always thought her mom enjoyed shocking people. She wore outrageous outfits full of color and frill whenever the urge struck her. She loved the attention whether it was good or bad. "I guess I got it from my Momma!" Goldie said to herself. "This world we live in is an amazing place." Her mom would say. "If you really think about it, its magic. They call it science, but I call it magic. The way things just work in harmony with each other." So, when a ten-year-old Goldie then known as Charles told her he was a girl she was thrilled. You see, baby. Life gave me a son and a daughter in all in one! What could be more magical than that?!" she exclaimed "Now are you sure, honey?" She asked. "Yes Momma. I'm not like the other boys. I don't want to run around throwing balls and rocks." she said. "Okay baby. I trust you know who you are. You just know that you don't have to stick to any one definition of who you are. Every day is an opportunity to do something else or be someone else. It's completely up to you!" her mother said. "Now, I love you no matter who you decide to be, but the rest of the world may not be as accepting." "I know" she said sadly. "Some boys make fun of me. They call me sissy." she said. The next week, she was enrolled in karate class. Her mom had known homosexual men and the bullies that preyed on them and knew that she would have to protect herself one day. In public, she still had to dress like a boy (it was the 70's after all) but at home she was free to dress as she pleased and be herself. Her mom passed away when she was in college. She missed her everyday. She laid back down and let those sweet memories undo the feelings left over by the dream. Today was a big day!

In the other room Misty was also trying to summon up some positive vibes. Today was the day! Misty was a designer and she had been asked to design the costumes for a show at Flame. Flame was a cabaret club where Goldie worked and was part owner. Misty started out just helping around the club. She had a flare for fashion, so when the performers started asking for tips, she fell right into place. She would help them select accessories and then she designed a headdress for Renee. Everybody loved it! After that, the performers would ask her to help them from time to time, but this was her first time designing for an entire show. Well, almost that was. Geraldo didn't want to wear her designs. "My tailor is the best and there was no way Misty could top his work." He said, "No shade." he said to Misty. "None taken." she replied, rolling her eyes. Geraldo was a diva in every since of the horrible little word. But she wasn't worried. These designs were her absolute best and after tonight he would beg her to design for him.

2

Misty wasn't Goldie's biological daughter, but she didn't think any daughter had ever loved their mother more than she loved Goldie. Misty grew up in the foster care system on Long Island. Bouncing from house to house is where she gained her appreciation of an outstanding performance. Each family wanted a different kid. She tried to be what each one wanted. The better her acting, the longer she stayed. Unfortunately, she was also witness to some terrible performances. She watched adults pretend to adore the children they fostered in front of the social workers. Then treat them like shit after the social worker left. Misty was never adopted, and older kids are harder to place. So, the bouncing eventually stopped. She had gotten used to the fact that she would be staying in the orphanage until she was 18. She was 14 at the time and figured 4 years wasn't so bad. Then she would be off to college or travel or whatever, but she'd be free to make her own decisions.

Her plans were blown to shit one night when she accepted an invite from a boy she liked. He asked her to hang out with him and his friends. She thought there would be other girls there, but she was the only one. They raped and beat her so badly that she could hardly walk. Bleeding and half blind, she dragged herself back to the orphanage. She was taken to the hospital and the police were called. She told them what had happened and who had done it. When the police went to question the boys, their parents lied and said they'd been together at home all night. They were from local families, so no one would believe her over them. They weren't even taken in for questioning. She stayed in the hospital for 3 weeks. Nobody came to visit her except her social worker and the police. They kept asking her what really happened. She kept repeating her story, and eventually they stopped coming. One night she overheard the nurses saying that they thought she was a prostitute, and a John had beaten her. Did they really think she was a prostitute? There was no way she could go back to the orphanage now. Life there was hard enough without them thinking you were a prostitute. So, the night before they released her from the hospital, she ran away. One nurse was nice. She gave her some clothes from the lost and found. She could see in her eyes that she knew what Misty was planning. She found $100 and a note that read "Good Luck!" in one of the pockets. She took it as a sign that things would be alright.

A fourteen year old runaway with one hundred dollars to her name, she knew she couldn't stay in town. So she went to the only place she could think of. She took the Long Island Railroad into the city. Misty sat by a window with her face covered. The conductor paused when he came to check her ticket. "Are you alone?" he asked. "Yes, my mom dropped me off and my dad is meeting me at the station." Misty answered. "Okay, let me know if you need help with anything." He replied. "Thank you." Misty said, still covering her face. She had never been to the city before and when she walked out of Penn Station, she felt like she had just taken a spaceship to mars. There were so many people around, even at 10:00 at night. She looked up and froze. Everything was so bright and so loud! There were people talking, music playing, horns honking, and there was a hum. She had never heard anything like it before. There was a vibration that seemed to connect every person to everything. She watched two men argue. There was a group of girls not much older than her dressed in party clothes. Were they out alone? Nobody seemed to care that she covered her face with her hoodie or notice her bandages. She walked for a while, just taking in the sights and sounds and smells that only Manhattan could produce. She got a slice of pizza and a soda and wandered into an alley to sit for a minute. It was filthy, but quiet. She sat on a piece of cardboard behind a dumpster and closed her eyes.

She had really done it! Now she had to come up with a plan. The money she had wouldn't last long. She heard a commotion coming her way. A guy was pushing a woman into her alley. "I told you that's all I got!" The woman said. "Bitch, stop playing with me. I saw you go to the ATM." The man growled. "Yeah, and that's all I took out. I just needed $20." the woman replied. The man slapped her, and she fell to the ground. He grabbed her purse and started going through it. Misty was terrified, but when she saw the man kick the woman, she knew she had to do something. If only someone would've been around to help her, she thought. She grabbed a brick from a pile she was using as a table and threw it at the man. It hit him in the middle of his back. When he turned around, another brick hit him in the face. His nose exploded in a flash of blood. He dropped the woman's purse and ran away, cursing about his revenge. The woman sat up against a wall while Misty gathered her belongings and put them back in the bag. She made sure her hoodie stayed over her face. "Thank you honey!" the woman said. "Thank God you were here! That's why I don't go to random ATMs, but this idiot said his card reader wasn't working. It was probably a setup. Goddam thieves!! But honey, what are you doing in this alley?" she asked, getting to her feet. "I just sat down to eat and…" Misty trailed off. "Eat? Here? Oh, honey. Are you homeless? God bless your heart! And that's quite a brave lil heart you have there too! Girl, I do not know what would've happened if you hadn't stepped up. Thank you, Lord!! Lord, I'm rambling! Okay well come on now. Let's go." She finally stopped talking. "Go? Go where?" Misty asked.

Honey, I'm not leaving you out here alone. Yes, you're brave and all, but what kind of woman would I be if I left the poor homeless girl that saved my life in this alley? I'm Goldie and you are?" Misty thought about it for a minute. She didn't know if they would put out a missing report on her. She guessed they had. "Darlene." she said. Goldie gave her a wayward look but said, "Okay Darlene, let's go." Misty looked back at her now cold pizza. Goldie said "Oh girl don't worry about that Momma Goldie is gonna feed you honey! You saved me and that's the least I can do!" That's what she said out loud, but she thought to herself "You saved me and now I'm gonna save you."

Misty pulled her hood lower when they walked into the diner. She could see people looking at her, but nobody seemed too concerned. She followed Goldie to a booth in the back. "What'll you have?" asked a waitress. "Give us a minute." Goldie replied. "So, what you wanna eat, Hun?" she asked Misty. Misty shrugged

"Pancakes" she said. Goldie got the waitress's attention and gave her their order. "So, how'd you end up in that alley Hun?" Goldie asked. "I don't wanna talk about it." Misty said. She could feel Goldie's stare, but she didn't ask any more questions. They ate in silence and when they were done Goldie asked, "You got some place to go?" Misty just shook her head. Well, you can stay at my place if you want. You're not on drugs, are you? "No!" Misty said quickly." "Okay. Cause I do not play that shit. And no stealing either. I don't have much but I'm willing to share. All you gotta do is ask." They left the diner and Goldie hailed a taxi. Goldie had a three-bedroom apartment near Christopher St. She gave Misty a quick tour and sat down on the couch. "Come here." She motioned Misty over. "I don't believe in coincidences. You and I were supposed to meet tonight. I'm not gonna ask you what happened to your face or what you're running from, except to say that if you're in some kind of legal trouble, you need to tell me now." Misty shook her head. "Okay then. You can stay as long as you need. Now you go get cleaned up and I'll give you something to sleep in." Goldie said. When she appeared at the bedroom door with the gown, Misty still had her hood on. "You can take that off now. There's peroxide and clean bandages in the bathroom. Like I said, I won't ask no questions. You'll tell me when you're ready." Misty looked at her but said nothing. "Goodnight child. I am tired! Who knew getting beat up could make you so tired" Goldie said as she walked away. She wondered exactly what had happened to this child, but she said nothing as she went to her room. When she said her prayers, she thanked God for the angel that He sent to her that night and wondered again who had saved who.

Misty slept in her clothes and when she got up the next morning, she put her shoes on and was planning to sneak out of the apartment, but when she opened the door the most wonderful aroma filled her nostrils. Goldie was already awake and from the looks of things, she had been for a while. She had cooked a breakfast feast. "For my guardian angel!" She said when she saw Misty. "I figured you might try to slide out unnoticed, so I got up early and honey, I don't do early for just anybody." Misty's stomach growled and her mouth watered. The food smelled amazing! "I know you only let me stay because I helped you, but you didn't have to do this. I don't want to be a bother." Misty said, staring at the food. Goldie looked at her sad bandaged face and her heart broke for this child. "Have a seat, child. I told you last night, we were put together for a reason. You clearly need a place to stay and someone to care for you. How old are you, 15?" she asked. "14" replied Misty, now sitting down. She looked at Goldie. Really looked at her. Something was different about this woman. Goldie noticed and said, "Honey have you ever seen a transexual before?" "Not in person." Misty replied. "Well, now, you have. Where are you from, child?" she asked. "Long Island" Misty said. "I ran away because of this." She motioned towards her face. "Before they could send me back to the group home. I can't go back there!" Goldie fought back tears. "What happened to this child?" she thought to herself. "I meant what I said last night. You can stay as long as you like. Do you want to stay?" she asked. Misty nodded. "Okay, all I ask is that when you decide you're ready to move out, you let me know so I'm not sitting here worrying about you. Okay?" Misty nodded. "Okay, now that that's settled, let's eat! Then we're going shopping. I noticed you didn't have any bags." Goldie said, getting the silverware out of a drawer. "I don't have much money." Misty said. "No worries, child. We're not going to Bloomingdales or anything. I do my best shopping at thrift stores and it's my treat!" That was 10 years ago. She went home with Goldie that night and never left. She had finally been adopted. Goldie was the mother she'd been praying for.

A few weeks after she moved in with Goldie, they were on the couch watching a movie. Something about it triggered a memory of a family that she lived with some years ago. They had been really good to her, and she hoped she would stay with them. The wife, Ms. Jones, was very sweet, and she cooked every day. There was always more than enough to eat. Mr. Jones was great with the boys. They played sports and went fishing all the time. She was invited too, but she just loved being around Ms. Jones. She was there for 7 months, and it was great!! One day they called everyone together and told them they had to move. Mr. Jones had accepted a position in another country and because they hadn't legally adopted them, they couldn't take them. Just like that, the fairy tale was over.

She told Goldie about the Jones', and she kept talking and talking until she got to that night. She told her how cute Ryan was and how much she liked him. She told her the whole story. Goldie quietly cried as she listened. Misty also cried. Not because of her own pain, but because she saw Goldie's tears. She believed her. She was the first person who did. None of the doctors, nurses, police or her social worker believed her. They all thought she was a prostitute. That nearly killed her. All these adults who were supposed to take care of her did exactly the opposite. The rape kit would have proved she was telling the truth, but as far as she knew, the boys had never been tested. When she found out that she'd be discharged she knew she had to run away. She knew she couldn't stay in that town.

3

The beating left her disfigured, and she was a runaway, so she never went back to school. She took GED classes online though and when she was 18, she took the GED exam and passed. By then, it didn't matter if her name got flagged in the system. She was a legal adult. She worked part time at Flame. Nobody there seemed to mind her appearance. They all accepted her for who she was. She had taken some fashion classes online and seemed to have a genuine talent for designing. She loved it there. She didn't have to hide or cover her face.

As a welcome to adulthood and graduation gift, Goldie and the girls at the club presented her with a check to pay for her reconstructive surgery. She stared at the check for a long time. She had dreamed about one day being able to get plastic surgery, but she didn't think it would ever really happen. It was crazy expensive, and she really didn't know if her face could be fixed. She had a collapsed eye socket, a crooked nose, and multiple scars on her face. She had more scars on her body, but those weren't visible in clothes, and she never wore short sleeves and forget about a bathing suit. To be able to walk outside with her head held high and face the world. To be a part of the world, not just an observer. She cried and cried. "Stop now" Goldie said "You're gonna make us cry and the last thing you wanna see is a bunch of drag queens in runny makeup!" Misty laughed wiping away her tears "Thank you all so much! I can't believe you did this for me!"

A few months later she had the operation and when the bandages came off, she was amazed!! The doctor didn't just fix her face. He grafted the scars on her face and arms. She was in bandages for weeks and she didn't go out the entire time. Seeing her face in bandages again was harder than she thought it would be, but it was worth it. The doctor hadn't just fixed her face. He made her beautiful! Like Kardashian beautiful! When she walked into the club that night, no one recognized her. She got makeup tips from Goldie. She still had faint scars, but foundation covered that. She'd never worn mascara or eyeliner because they didn't allow that at the group home. And after that night, she didn't see the point. Now she loved it. It was amazing how a small amount could transform the way you looked.

The next year was amazing! She dated, she danced, and she sang (in public). She laughed and smiled more than she had in her entire life. Her new life was perfect. She really enjoyed dating until they tried to get intimate. She would come up with an excuse and end things shortly after. The surgery had fixed her outside, but she didn't know if anything could fix her internal scars. They had taken so much from her that night. They had nearly taken her life, and what happened to them? "Nothing, not a fucking thing!" Mistry seethed. They needed to pay for what they did to her. She didn't know how, but she'd make them pay. Over the next few months, she researched her attackers and found that they all lived in the city too. No real surprise there. That was one of the things she'd planned with Ryan. Once she knew where they were, she started working on a plan and now she was here on a date with Paul.

Once she'd found her attackers online, she did a deep dive into their lives. Maybe that night had been the only time they'd done something like that. Maybe they were good men that made a horrible mistake as kids. Nope. She found an article from a few years after she'd left that said they'd been accused and questioned about an attack. This girl was from a local family, so the cops had taken it more seriously. But their parents covered for them again and there was no rape, so there was no DNA. So, it was just her word against theirs. They hadn't changed. They'd done it again. Who knows how many times? She made up her mind. She started reading true crime books and watching forensic shows. If she was going to do this, she damn sure wasn't going to get caught. It was always the small things that got people caught. She'd have to have a plan. Her besties Ralph and Renee questioned her new obsession, but she told them it was research for a book she was writing. That satisfied them. They knew what had happened to her and thought maybe victims found comfort in knowing they weren't the only victims in the world.

When Misty decided to start her surveillance, she borrowed a wig from one of the girls at the club and went out as a different person. The first one she decided to make contact with was Paul. He stopped at the supermarket every Friday evening after work. She was just going to walk past him a few times, maybe ease drop on his phone call, but no contact, not now. It was all going according to plan until she knocked over a display of macaroni and he came to help. Her breath stopped when she looked up and saw him kneeling there. Did he recognize her? Did he remember those eyes that pleaded with him to stop? "I don't know why they put these things here. Somebody knocks them down at least twice a week." He said, handing her a can of tuna. She looked at him and finally took a breath when she realized he didn't recognize her. She giggled absently. "Yeah, they probably like watching people bump into it." She took her tuna and turned to walk away. "So, what's your name?" he asked. "Huh? Oh um. I gotta go." She stammered and walked away. She left the basket at the front and left the store. She hadn't intended on speaking to him. She didn't know what to say when he asked for her name. "He really didn't recognize me?" She said to herself. How could he not know who she was? Yes, her face was different but still. She thought something like that would leave a lasting memory. I guess it depends on which part you played in the story. That night was burned into her mind forever. She'd often heard of victims not having any memory of their attack. She always thought they were lucky. When she calmed down, she realized that this was a good thing. If they didn't recognize her, they'd never see her coming.

A waiter dropped his tray, and the noise jolted her back to the present. He was talking about work. She told him a funny story she'd heard on the train. They laughed and drank. She drank just enough to appear tipsy. She had to stay in control tonight. She didn't want to fuck this up and have to go on another date with him. Tonight, she would know if she could actually do what she'd planned. If she could kill, commit murder, take another human being's life. Killing someone by accident was one thing. Anybody was capable of that given the right or wrong circumstances. This was different. She figured that if she got through this first one, she would be able to get through the rest of them. She hoped that was the case. She didn't want to pray that the murder went well. It didn't seem right, but she could hope.

When they left the restaurant, they walked a bit. It was cold but beautiful. He invited her back to his place, and she accepted. She'd watched so many "True Crime" shows that she felt like an expert, but the closer they got the more her nerve seemed to fade. She debated for the trillionth time if she could really do this. He deserved it, they all deserved it. They deserved to die and be brought back just to die over and over again for all eternity as far as she was concerned. But could she be the one to do it? She'd fantasized about it every day since that night. She was so naïve to think that he liked her. Ryan. She'd had different fantasies then. Her and Ryan sitting in a tree, K I S S I N G. She'd only gone into the woods because of him. He'd played her so well. She brought herself back. "Can't get distracted." She thought. She'd see Rayan soon enough, but tonight was all about Paul. She took his hand. He squeezed hers as they crossed the street.

When they got to his apartment Misty excused herself and went to the bathroom. She looked at her reflection in the bathroom mirror and gave herself one last pep talk. "You can do this. He deserves this." She closed her eyes and steadied herself. He was sitting on the couch and there were 2 glasses of wine on the table. She took a glass but didn't sit down. She walked behind him and bent over and kissed his cheek. She picked up the bottle and said, "let's get comfortable" as she walked toward his bedroom. When her back was to him, she slipped belladonna in the bottle. Belladonna is a plant that can be used as a sedative. When used in small doses, it's harmless, but when used in large doses, it can be deadly. She used just enough to knock him out. No, there would be no easy out for this guy. She wasn't sure how much she could take, but she was going to make him hurt. She filled his glass and as he drank the wine, she began to take her clothes off. He put the glass down to join her, but she stopped him. "No, baby, just watch". she said seductively. He laid back and continued drinking his wine. She danced to the music and wondered again if she was really going to go through with this. She could leave with the superior feeling of knowing that she had complete control over this man's life. Would that be enough? Could she live with that?

Misty knew she had to be mindful of surveillance cameras. They were everywhere and many people got caught because of them. Earlier at dinner, she mentioned that she was thinking of getting one and asked if he had any suggestions. He said he didn't have any, but she checked anyway. She also checked his phone for an app. Nope, nothing there. Perfect!

When Paul fell asleep, she undressed him. He mumbled a bit at first, but soon he was completely knocked out. As she stood there looking at his naked body, she had flashbacks of that night. The things he'd said and done to her. How he'd laughed when the other boys took their turn. She felt tears run down her cheeks. Was she crying? "No, no, no!" she scolded herself. No DNA left behind. She got the spray bottle she'd filled with bleach and sprayed the area. When Paul saw her carrying a large bag, he smiled. He probably assumed it was an overnight bag. She laughed at the thought. The bag contained what she called her anti-CSI kit. It contained bleach, gloves, semen, and hair she'd collected at her other job. Through her research, she learned that every hair and drop of biological fluid found at a crime scene was tested for DNA. She knew that being careful could only get her so far, so she decided to be messy. She got a job at a Dominatrix club. It was easy with her new face. The things they did in that place were not for the faint of heart. It was also research of a different kind. She figured eventually she would meet someone she did want to have sex with, so she took notes on how the ladies looked at the men and how they spoke. She had never tried to be seductive before, but judging by Paul's response, she guessed she was good at it. She had all the samples her vengeful little heart desired. She didn't want anyone getting in trouble for her crimes, so she decided she'd use so much that the police would figure it must be a mistake. Plus, if they managed to track the guys down, they'd never admit to being a member of the club, so they still wouldn't have a connection. She was still contaminating the scene when Paul started to wake up. She sat next to him and waited for him to feel the restraints on his wrists and ankles and the gag she'd put in his mouth. She stood, and he looked at her naked body and tried to smile. She'd undressed so she wouldn't get blood on her clothes. His face darkened when he saw her scars. "You like?" she asked, turning around like she was modeling new clothes. He shook his head as he tried to speak. She took the gag out of his mouth. "What happened to you? Look, if you're into devil worship or something, you can just leave. I just wanted some fun."

"Devil worship? I guess you could say that. I fell for the wrong guy, and he was evil." She gestured toward her body. He and his friends did this. Don't you remember? Oh, that's right, you probably wouldn't remember exactly where you cut me. It was so long ago and there was so much blood." She said. "What are you talking about? I didn't do that to you! Okay that's it. Untie me. You're nuts and I'm over this" He began jerking at his restraints.

"Oh, you did this alright," she said as she walked over and placed the gag back in his mouth. "You and Kevin, and Sean, and Ryan." She said.

"Yes!" she said when realization appeared in his eyes. "That's right. It's me. I'm back!" she said mockingly. "Now, do you remember? Of course, you do. Who could forget the night they beat and raped and almost killed an innocent girl that just wanted to be your friend!" she was screaming now. She took a breath and steadied herself. When she spoke again, she was more composed. Paul was shaking his head violently now. She removed the gag again. "You, you, you can't be. You can't be her!" he stammered. "Oh yes! It's me!" She said as she put the gag back. He tried to bite her, and she slapped him. Hitting him felt good! "I know you have questions, Paul. The short answer is that doctors these days can fix just about anything. What you and your friends did to me" her voice trailed off as she was taken back to that night. "I just wanted to be friends." She was crying again. "The things you did to me. I could barely walk. You almost killed me! Was that the plan? Kill me so I couldn't tell anyone what you did? Well, it didn't matter because you lied, and your parents lied. They say if you lie, you'll steal. You lied, and you stole. You stole my childhood, my happiness, my face, and my body!!" She was screaming again. She had grabbed the knife out of her bag. When he saw it, he started to plead with her. "I'm sorry!! We were just kids. We didn't mean for it to go like that. It just got out of hand." "Out of hand? Out of hand? Are you fucking kidding me? Oops we slipped and raped you. Oops we didn't mean to bash your face in. Oops we didn't mean to stab and slice up your body!" She was screaming again as she drove the knife into his thigh. He screamed. She quickly covered his face with a pillow. She had planned on putting the muffle in his mouth so his screams wouldn't be heard but hearing it was so satisfying. Now he knew what she felt all those years ago. Scared and in pain. Praying for someone to save you.

Her plan was to torture him all night, but when she removed the knife, she knew she'd messed up. There was too much blood! She'd hit his femoral artery. He'd be dead soon. Too soon. "Dam, dam, dam!!" she said to herself. But as she watched the terrified tears roll down his face, she grew calm. Yes, death was coming sooner than she planned, but he knew. He knew why. He knew who she was and that she'd done this to him. She'd scold herself later. It was her first murder, after all. Didn't everybody make mistakes their first time? She stood over him and said, "you're just the first. I know where your friends are, and I have plans for them, too. He tried to speak again and then his eyes closed and he was gone.

She looked at him a while longer. She was waiting to feel something, but nothing came. "Dam" she thought. They had broken her. Only a monster could do this and not feel anything. "Well, I guess it takes a monster to kill a monster." she said. She sprayed his body with bleach again before getting to work on the apartment. When she left, she said good night to the doorman. She didn't try to hide her face because it never worked and just made you look more conspicuous. She looked exactly like she did when she walked in with him. They'd try to find her, but she didn't exist, so hey. She strolled across the street into Central Park and Paul's date vanished forever.

Paul lived on 90th St and 5th Ave. His address was perfect. She knew it wouldn't be this easy again. She walked through the park for about a half mile and dipped into a nook she'd picked out during a recon mission. When she was mapping out her escape plan, she found a lot of articles about surveillance in the park. There had been a lot of reports of outraged victims of various crimes that took place in areas that were digital blind spots. She'd placed her getaway bag under a bush weeks ago and come back to check on it at different times of the day to see if it had been taken or gone through.

She dipped behind the bush and removed her disguise, coat, and shoes. She changed into athletic clothes and sneakers. She had one of those puffer jackets that folded up into a little wallet. "Boy, these things really come in handy." She said to herself. She put everything in a backpack and walked out of the park as a brunette in running gear. She'd dispose of the murder clothes later. She did not need some homeless person walking around in that outfit covered in her DNA. She exited the park on 110th St and entered the subway station.

4

It had all gone as planned. Well, almost. He didn't die the way she planned, but he was dead. And he knew who she was and why she'd done it. She didn't know how she felt. She'd wondered for so long if she could actually do it. Was she that person? Yeah, she was that person. The person who took back her life from the men that had stolen it. The person who got revenge. As she boarded the train, she felt a surge of confidence, like she'd never felt. If she could do this, she could do anything. This was the beginning of her new life. Once she killed the other three, she'd take over the world!! She laughed out loud at the thought. She boarded the train and was so engrossed in her thoughts that she didn't notice a guy approaching her. When she looked up and saw him, she screamed. "I'm sorry. I'm sorry." He said. She couldn't breathe. How did they find her?

Did they see her change in the park? "Shit! Shit! Shit! Shit!" She said to herself. She exited the train at 14th St on wobbly legs. When she saw he had gotten off too, she almost fainted. She sat down on the bench because there was no way she could outrun them. She would've put her hands up for him to slap the cuffs on, but she couldn't move. "I'm sorry, did I scare you? Are you ok?" he asked, seeing the shock in her face. "I just wanted to talk to you. I saw you get on the train and you're so beautiful I just had to speak to you!" He said looking embarrassed. She was still staring at him. When she didn't reply he said, "I'm sorry to bother," and walked away.

When her brain realized what was going on and she could breathe again, she laughed with relief. She couldn't stop laughing. She was so sure that she had been caught that she was about to make a full confession. When she composed herself, she ran to catch up with him and explain. He was handsome and embarrassed. She touched his shoulder. "I'm sorry. I'm not laughing at you. Whoa, give me a second" she said holding up her hand and trying to reign in the laughter. He was relieved to see that she wasn't rejecting him. "Hi

I'm Misty." She said, "I'm so sorry. I was completely lost in my thoughts. You nearly scared me to death." She said, finally able to stop laughing and speak in full sentences. "Hello, I'm Troy! And I'm sorry for scaring you. Let me make it up to you. How about lunch?" he said. "Lunch? Its almost 10." She giggled. "I meant tomorrow," he said, smiling.

They talked a little more as they waited for the next train. He apologized a few more times and so did she. They agreed on a place and time and exchanged numbers. He texted her about 30 minutes later. It was just a heart emoji. She stared at the phone and smiled. She didn't return his text.

The first thing she did when she got home was to get in the shower. She stood there and let the hot water run over her body for a long time. She had actually done it. She'd killed him. She'd made a plan, stuck to it, and it worked. And then she got a date! Dam he was cute! "Oh no, girl. You cannot let that man distract you." She scolded herself. "Business first and then daydreams." she still had to get rid of the disguise and murder kit. She didn't want to use the same samples for each murder. That would definitely be a connection the cops would follow up on.

She wondered how long it would take for them to find him. She could picture the headlines and the article full of lies from his family and friends about what a great guy he was and how he was such a sweet kid. Her thoughts went back to Troy. Dam he was cute. And that smile! Boy, oh boy, what crazy timing. She wondered why she'd run after him like that. She guessed it was the leftover confidence and adrenaline. She'd been so consumed with her revenge plan that she hadn't even thought about dating. It would be nice to have someone to talk to. Yes, she had the twins and Goldie, but it wasn't the same. She got into bed and drifted to sleep with thoughts of sex. She didn't know if it was killing Paul or meeting Troy that brought up these urges, but it scared her. Of all the things she thought she'd feel after committing murder, hot and horny wasn't on the list at all. Was she a monster?

She woke up to the smell of breakfast cooking and the sounds of laughter. Goldie was cooking, and the twins were cackling. This typical for a Saturday morning. Since they were all so busy, Goldie insisted on a family breakfast once a month. "Late night, huh?" Ralph asked. "Did you get lucky?" He asked the same question after every date. He was convinced she had a secret lover. He said there was no way she was single in this town with that face and body. "Shit, I'd considered switching sides for you." He said jokingly.

"What's for breakfast?" she asked. Ignoring him. "Breakfast Tacos!" Goldie said as she kissed her forehead. "Yes!" exclaimed Ralph and Renee in unison. Breakfast tacos were their favorite. Breakfast tacos were scrambled eggs with shrimp and veggies folded in a pancake. Renee was saying something, but no one could understand him with his mouth full. He always talked with food in his mouth. "As a matter of fact, I did meet someone." She blushed as she gave them the details. She left out the part about the murder. "He sent a text last night and this morning, and I'm meeting him for brunch." She said, snapping her fingers. "Oh shit! I don't think I've ever seen you blush like this," Goldie said. "Well, I'm glad you're eating now." Renee said. "You never want to go on a first date hungry! You'll either eat everything on your plate or you'll sit there with your stomach growling so loud it'll seem like it's a third person on your date." he shuddered as they all burst into laughter. Misty turned to Goldie and asked, "How was your night?" "Just marvelous darling" she said in her best British accent. "I sang, I danced, I lit up the room as usual!" Ralph grabbed Goldie's hand and the two began dancing around the room. Misty watched them and smiled. Sometimes she couldn't believe this was her life. She was truly blessed! How could a life that started out so shitty, become this beautiful? Her phone buzzed. It was Troy again. "That must be him. Girl, you better not ever enter a poker tournament." Renee said, poking her in the arm. "I can't help it. He's so..." Misty paused searching for the right word. "Yummy!" "Yummy?" the others said in unison. They had never heard her talk about anybody that way. "Girl, you gotta get that under control before your date. You gotta make him work for it!" Ralph said. "I know!" Misty said. "Help me." She said as she fell back onto the couch. "First thing you do is ignore that call. Wait a few minutes before you call him back." Goldie said. "You have to set the control settings on Misty! Let there be no mistake about who's running things." "But..." Misty said, reaching for the phone as it stopped buzzing. "She's right." Renee said "You have to train them right from the start. Just like puppies."

"Okay, let's get u dressed." Said Ralph. "I can dress myself." Misty said, laughing. "Yes, but you're nervous and you'll rethink everything you choose. It'll take way too long to long to decide and you'll end up picking something out of frustration." Said Renee. "And that's never good." Said Goldie. "You like him, and you want to look good, so let them help you. You'll be confident in your look, and we all know" she paused and pointed at them. "Confidence is your best accessory" they all said in unison. Goldie had beat that into their heads. Confidence will get you in the door, but cockiness will get you kicked out." She would say. She talked to Misty about things like that every day.

Before her surgery, she had no confidence. Goldie slowly helped her find things that she was good at. Art and fashion were what she excelled at. Goldie said, "Honey, the way you look is only a small part of who you are. The fashions you create are works of art! Your art will tell people who you are before they ever meet you. Be confident in your art and it will spread. When you walk out that door, you'll carry an air of confidence that people will feel. Then if you decide to let them see your face, it won't matter." Slowly, she became more confident, and it was just like Goldie predicted. Nobody ran away when they saw her face. In fact, that had been how she'd met the twins. She was on the train when Ralph complemented her on her shoes. Then Renee asked about her jacket. They didn't seem fazed by her looks or shyness at all. They just kept talking. She hadn't said a word other than thank you, but they hadn't noticed. She laughed. A little at first, but then it became a big belting laugh. They looked stunned at first, like they just remembered she was there. Then they laughed too. She couldn't remember the last time she'd laughed that hard. It felt good. Really good. When they stopped laughing, they introduced themselves. Misty had been on her way to buy some fabric. They joined her and she'd been stuck with them ever since. Ralph and Renee weren't really twins. They met at a pride event in Washington Heights. Their outfits were similar, so they kept calling the other twin. They did it so much that people assumed they were actual twins. Ralph was a receptionist for a PR firm in midtown and Renee worked in the shoe department at Bloomingdales. They lived in Renee's Grandmother's apartment in a NYCHA development on 26th St. When she introduced them to Goldie, it was love at first sight and they'd been family ever since.

Goldie also warned her about becoming over, confident. She didn't think that would ever happen. Every look in the mirror was humbling. She knew the world would never fully accept her with that face. Now that she had a new face, she remained humble, in part because of Goldie's lessons, but mostly because she still didn't feel beautiful. Sometimes she was surprised by her reflection. Sometimes it felt like a mask. She would watch beautiful women and try to mimic their mannerisms. She admired the way they held their heads high and looked people directly in the eyes when they talked.

On her way out the door she sent a group text to Goldie and the twins with Troy's name, number, and where they were meeting. This was their routine when going out with a new person.

Safety first, love second. There were too many cases of dates going wrong and nobody having enough info to give to the cops. She would take a pic with him and send that to them later. Misty checked her reflection in a store window as she approached the restaurant. The guys had been right. Nothing she had tried to put together felt right. They decided for her, and she must admit they had done well. Her stomach was doing flips that got worse as she got closer. "What is going on?" she thought. She hadn't liked anyone this much in a long time. She'd only seen and spoken to him once but what an impression he'd made. She had to play this cool. She checked her reflection once more before going in.

5

He was sitting at a table by the window. "Dam he was good looking!" she thought. He was dressed in jeans, a peach button-up shirt and a navy-blue blazer. Misty wondered if he had trouble picking an outfit. She giggled at the thought. He stood up when he saw her. "You look amazing!" he said with a big smile. "Let me help you with your coat." He draped her coat on the back of her chair and pulled it out for her almost at the same time. "I'm so happy you agreed to meet me. I'm really sorry that I scared you last night. I didn't want you to get off the train before I had a chance to speak to you. Had I known we were getting off at the same stop, I probably would've been a little smoother." he said, blushing a little. While he was talking, Misty was chanting, "Be cool. Be cool." Over and over in her head. "Thank you!" she said as she took her seat. "Don't worry about it. I'm just glad you weren't a creep. I was so lost in thought that I really didn't see you. I'm not usually that bad." She giggled nervously. "It's okay! You might have walked the other way if you'd seen me coming," he said with a smile. The waiter showed up, and they ordered drinks and appetizers. "So, Misty, huh? I guess your parents were big Clint Eastwood fans." When he saw the puzzled look on her face, he asked, "You've heard of him, haven't you?" "Yeah, but what's he got to do with my name?" she asked. "Play Misty For Me is one of his biggest movies! I can't believe nobody ever told you that." he said. "A movie? Had she really named herself after a movie and not known it? Good grief, girl!" Misty thought, shaking her head.

Misty was born Michelle April Jones. "It's a good name." She'd heard the lady at the foster home say. "At least it isn't Laquanisha or Oceanicca or some other God, awful name like that." The lady said. "She won't have to change it to get a job." At the time, Misty hadn't understood what the lady was talking about. Those names seemed better that Michelle. Later on, Misty learned that the practice of naming children these exquisitely different names began during slavery. Parents would do this so that if they're children were sold to another family they would be able to identify them if they ever crossed paths again. When she moved to the city, she loved walking in the park on misty days. She loved to feel the floating mist on her face. A few weeks after her surgery, Goldie asked her how she felt. "I'm okay! Not much pain at all." Misty answered. "No, that's not what I mean. How do you feel on the inside? You have this new face. You've been out a few times. How do you feel?" Goldie said. "Oh. Umm I guess I feel okay." Misty said. "Just, okay?" Goldie asked. Misty thought about it for a few minutes. "I guess I do feel different. I went outside yesterday without my face covered but I didn't realize it till I saw my reflection in the store window. I reached for my hoodie before I realized I hadn't worn it. I just stared at myself for a second and then I walked in." She looked at Goldie with tears in her eyes. "Thank you!!" Goldie hugged her gently. "I've noticed a change in you. You are not that same little shy child anymore. Have you thought about changing your name?" "Why would I do that? Can I do that?" Misty asked. "Yes girl! There is so much in a name. Why do you think all of us Queens change our names? When you choose your own name, it gives it an unparalleled power! It announces to the world how you want the world to see you!" Goldie said.

Misty thought of that lady in the foster home and what she'd said. She understood it now. Would Laquanisha name herself that if it were up to her? "Misty" she said. Goldie leaned back and looked at her. "Oh yes honey! That's you!" Goldie said, hugging her again. "Misty what? What's your last name?" "I don't know. What's yours?" Misty replied. "My last name is Ramsey. I was going to change it, but I decided to keep it in honor of my mother." Well, I'll be Misty Ramsey. If that's okay with you." Goldie grabbed Misty and hugged her. "Of course, it's okay with me!" The next day, she applied for an official name change. Misty asked the attendant, "If someone looks up my old name will they find me?" "No honey. The only way they'll connect that name to you is if they have your social security number." She replied. "See I told you!" Goldie said. "Abusive ex?" asked the attendant. Goldie nodded. The attendant shook her head and said, "Let's get you taken care of honey!"

"I guess it's possible. I didn't know my parents. I grew up in foster care." she said shyly. "Oh man, I'm sorry. Me and my big mouth. I tend to ramble when I'm nervous." he said. "I make you nervous?" she asked, a little too enthusiastically. "Yeah, a little." he said, smiling. "I mean, look at you! You're gorgeous and you dress nicely! What guy wouldn't be nervous?" She was blushing again. Her entire face felt hot, so she started chanting again. "Be cool. Be cool. Be cool." He was looking at her like he was waiting for an answer. "I'm sorry, what did you say?" she asked. "I just said that maybe we could watch it together." He said "Maybe." She said "I'm sorry. I didn't get much sleep. I was up all night, working on some designs." "Oh, you're a designer? Clothes, right?" he asked, "How'd you know?" she asked, "Look at you!" He said "You look like you're going to a fashion show. Not in one. The models always look uncomfortable. You look like the people in the audience that look like money!" She laughed out loud. She knew exactly what he meant and the fact that she hadn't dressed herself made it even funnier. "You go to many fashion shows?" she asked once she stopped laughing. "I dated a model once. She wasn't one of the highly paid ones, but she did a lot of shows, and she always wanted me to go with her." He said, "Oh okay." she replied. She wanted to know if he was still dating her and if not, why. She always wondered why beautiful women were single. Did they rely on their looks too much? Were they boring or rude? Were men intimidated by them? "Questions for another day." She thought and shrugged. "So, what do you do?" she asked. "I'm a detective." He answered. Misty felt all the air leave her lungs as her heart stopped again. "A detective?" she said, willing her heart to stay in her chest. "Are you okay? You're not afraid of cops, are you?" he asked. "No, no, I just choked." She said, finding her breath again. "Oh, that's good. Not that you choked. I meant good, you're not afraid of cops." His entire face was red now. It made Misty feel better. He wouldn't be blushing if he was here to arrest her. "I've met women who refused to date a cop. They said it was too stressful. That's what happened with the model I told you about." he said, looking into his lap. "Well, that answers that." Misty thought. "Really? I've never met a cop before or anyone that's dated one, so I wouldn't have an opinion on that. You don't look like a detective, though." she said, motioning to his clothes. "Do you all dress this well?" she asked with genuine interest. He laughed a hearty laugh. "No, not at all. You wouldn't believe how much flack I get for the way I dress. They call me Detective GQ." He said using air quotes. They both laughed. She was happy that she'd successfully covered up her panic attack, and that he wasn't here to arrest her. Only she would run smack into a gorgeous cop that wanted to date her while she was in the middle of a murder spree. "WTF universe?" she thought.

She decided that since he wasn't trying to trick her into confessing over brunch, she would just enjoy herself. He was perfect. Except for that whole cop thing. She would finish their date and never see him again. How could she? She was one quarter of the way through her murder spree and dating anyone, especially a cop, would just complicate things. She had to finish what they started. It was the only way for her wounds to heal.

6

A week later, Misty was scrolling through the Post's website when she saw it. They had finally found Paul. The article was small. The building manager had found him after she received calls from his family and job. Detectives had no leads and were asking for anyone with information to come forward. "Ha!" she said. "A small article for a small man. I bet he thought he'd make the front page. Well, you thought wrong dick head!" she said, giggling.

The last week had been crazy! Her date with Troy had gone very well. They'd been texting and talking ever since and were going out again that night. She had been working on her designs for the show at the club and been setting up her next kill. Kevin was next. Kevin was a writer for The Times. He was pretty good, too. A few months ago, his girlfriend left him, which was perfect. Guys always felt like they had something to prove after a break-up. Like they had to show the world, they still had it. He was into serious types, so Misty became Cassandra, a Journalistic film student. Cassandra had long brown hair and wore glasses.   Misty had approached him previously as a redhead and he politely rejected her flirtations. He'd met Cassandra at Starbucks. She was pretending to have a conversation with someone about the content of their next piece and how great it would be if they could interview a writer from a major news outlet. It worked like a charm! They sat for a while and discussed world news and some of his articles. She told him about her film and thanked him many times for offering to be interviewed.   He flirted a little, but she pretended not to notice.   She had to be all business with this one if she was going to get close enough for her plan to work. She hadn't seen anything that indicated that he went for quick sex. He approached relationships like he did his articles. Research, then execute. She'd rented an Air B&B for a month and registered at the New School. Just in case he checked her story. She'd learned that you can never assume what someone will do, so when you create a cover, you create an entire life. No small lies, just one big one.

Goldie was at the club doing a pre-show check. She had worked and performed there as long as she could remember, but this was the first show she'd written and directed. She'd been working on it for years, but was too afraid to say anything. One night she told Misty about it and instantly regretted it until she looked up and saw that she was smiling from ear to ear. "I love it!" Misty said. "You do?!" asked Goldie. "Yes!" exclaimed Misty as she jumped up and hugged her. "I can already see it! I'll design all the outfits! We can help with the arrangements." "We?" Goldie asked. "We! Yes, we! The twins and me. You know they're going to beg to be in it. They can't act but you can let them audition." Misty said this as she started twirling around the room. Goldie and Misty went over the show many times. Misty offered her feedback and took notes. When she gave it to the girls at the club, they all loved it. Everyone wanted the lead role. They held auditions and after a few rather dramatic moments they had their cast. The twin's auditions were just what they expected, horrible, but they were happy when they were offered stagehand positions. That was 6 months ago, and tonight was the debut. She closed her eyes and said a prayer. She thanked God for Misty as she had done a million times before. That wonderful girl had shown up in her life and given her a purpose. She was truly a blessing.

The show was amazing! It was about a transgender man that was discovered at a local bar and quickly became a superstar. His mother and father had abandoned him when he transitioned but now wanted to be back in his life. After the show, Goldie was on top of the world! The audience really loved it! There were tears and laughter right where they were supposed to be. She couldn't believe this was her real life, so she pinched herself and laughed. She dedicated the performance to her best friend, Molly. Molly had been murdered by some anti-gay thugs that beat her to death. Her picture was in the center of a wall full of pictures of souls that had been taken too soon. She looked at her picture and could feel tears welling up in her eyes. Just then, she heard Molly's voice. "Oh, no Bitch! No tears in public. Runny make-up is never sexy!" Goldie burst out laughing in the empty room and said, "Okay! Okay! I know. Suck it up and spit it out!" That's what they always said about any ugliness the world threw at them. "You can't let it sit and fester or it will eat you alive. You suck that shit up and you spit it out!" She was brought back to reality by Renee calling her name. "Where were you, Mama?" He asked. "No time for drifting tonight. We got some celebrating to do!" he said as he twirled toward her and hugged her.

Misty woke up the next morning fully dressed and feeling like she'd taken on a gorilla. Everything hurt. She thought she could feel her hair growing and that hurt, too. She got up and took some Advil and drank a lot of water. She had to get herself together. She was having her first date with Kevin this afternoon. He had asked her out several times, but she kept declining. She was a busy student, after all. The date started at Met Museum. There was a new exhibit that he wanted to see. Romance in 19th century France. She giggled. He was really working hard. "Good!" she said under her breath. The exhibit was beautiful, and she really enjoyed it. She just wished she was seeing it with Troy instead of

Kevin. He'd called, but she didn't answer, of course. She'd tell him she was sleeping, after last night's party she should be sleeping, but the mission came first. As they were leaving, they walked past a medieval torture device and Misty said, "Wow, that looks like fun." Kevin's response made her pause. "Only if there's a safe word." "A safe word? Like what?" she asked. "Something simple. Like indigo. You know, anything will do." he replied as he continued to look at the device. His thoughts had clearly taken him to another place, and Misty knew exactly where that place was. This date had turned out to be very informative. When Kevin said indigo, she'd recognized his voice saying that word. He was a member of one of the sex clubs she worked at. His mistress was Mistress Rochelle.

Mistress Rochelle was tough on her subjects. Misty would always hear moans and cries of pleasure and pain coming from her dungeon. That was where she'd collected most of her anti-CSI kit. Luckily, Misty started working there after she killed Paul. She remembered indigo because he always started off low. Like he was bored. This made Mistress Rochelle hit him harder and harder until he was screaming. Misty couldn't believe it. This was perfect! She needed to change her plans, but this was going to be so much better. Misty should've seen this for the giant red flag that it was, but she was so focused on the plan that she didn't.

7

Troy's day wasn't going so well. He had been called out to a hit and run. Two guys who had been friends got into a fight and one ran the other over with his car. He hated these cases. He couldn't understand how you could hurt someone that you were friends with. "Friends are the family you choose." He always said. Yes, you could say the same for husband and wife, but many people got married for the wrong reasons and eventually things went bad. Friendships were usually built on mutual interests and if those interests change, you just stop being friends. There was something about marriage that made people forget they could just walk away. Why stay and torture each other when you can just leave? He'd seen friendships fall apart before, but when one of them turned to violence, it was usually about jealousy, a romantic rivalry or money. It constantly amazed him, the things that made people jealous. Drugs were also a reason, and sometimes number four led to numbers one and three. In this case there seemed to be a bit of all four.   The hitter was jealous of the victim and when he was high, he approached the victim's girlfriend and decided to tell her all the reasons she shouldn't be with the victim. This led to a fight and during the fight he got scared and hit the victim with his car. His toxicology report came back positive for several drugs. The victim was pretty banged up, but he'd survive. Troy was an only child, so he considered his friends his brothers and sisters. He didn't keep in contact with many of them anymore, but he couldn't imagine hurting any of them to that extent. He had gotten into a fight with Ryan when they were in college, but it was just a few punches. Truth be told, the fight made them closer.

He'd met Ryan on their first day of college, and it was like meeting his long-lost brother. Troy didn't feel like unpacking, so he went to the basketball court to shoot hoops. Ryan was there, but he didn't have a ball. Troy asked if he wanted to play one on one and the rest is history. Ryan was quiet, and a little withdrawn. Troy, on the other hand, was the life of the party. He didn't understand why Ryan was that way. He was good looking and good at sports. A regular chick magnet, but he barely paid them any attention. He didn't really want Troy around them, either. One day while they were eating, Troy asked the tough question. "Dude, are you gay?" he asked, "I'm not judging but I just want to know." Troy continued holding up his hands.

Ryan's face fell. He couldn't believe what he was hearing. "Hell no! Why would you ask me that? What? Do you think I want you or something?" Ryan yelled as he rose to leave. "Nah, it's not that. I don't get that vibe from you at all, but you never want to be around any girls, and it seems like you don't want me to be around them either. I don't get it." Ryan stopped at the door and when he turned around, Troy saw that he was crying. "Can I trust you?" he asked Troy. "Of course, Bro!" Troy answered. He didn't know what was happening, but Ryan was his friend, and he was clearly hurting. Ryan sat down and told Troy about the night of the attack. The night that changed his life. He had never spoken about that night to anyone. As he spoke, he cried a deep, cleansing cry. He cried for all they had lost that night and all they had taken. When he stopped talking, they just sat in silence for what seemed like forever. When Troy spoke, his voice cracked from holding in his own tears. "What happened to her?" he asked. "I don't know." Ryan answered. "How could you do that?" Troy asked. The look on his face was one of pure disgust. Ryan couldn't meet his eyes. "How could you do that? I thought you were solid man! How could you do that?" Troy was screaming as he jumped up and punched Ryan in the face. He kept hitting him until he realized Ryan wasn't fighting back. Troy fell back against his dresser and let his tears flow. They both cried themselves to sleep. The next morning, they woke up and stared at each other. "Now what?" Ryan asked. His eye was swollen, and his ribs were sore, but he figured he deserved the beating. It would've been worse if Troy wasn't outraged. Ryan didn't want to be friends with someone that wasn't outraged by what he'd done. When Troy spoke, his voice still cracked a little. "Tell me the truth. Did you touch her? Did you rape her?" "No, I told you I didn't touch her, but I didn't stop the others." Ryan said, with his head hanging low. "Have you tried to find out what happened to her?" Troy asked, raising his voice a little. "Yeah, I Google her name all the time! I've checked missing person reports and police blogs. It's like she disappeared when she left the hospital." Troy stood, and Ryan flinched. "I'm not going to hit you again. Sorry about that. I was so pissed and disappointed, you know? I thought you were a stand-up dude. I get it now though. Why you don't want to be around girls." He offered Ryan his hand and said, "We're going to find her." "We?" Ryan asked as he took Troy's hand. Troy helped him up and said, "Yeah, you gotta make this shit right, or at least die trying." "What if we can't find her?" Ryan asked. "Do you pray?" Troy asked Ryan. "Pray?" Ryan said looking puzzled. Troy said, "Look, you may not find her, but you still have to make things right within yourself. The only way to do that is to repent. You have to ask God for forgiveness and earn it with your actions. Staying away from girls and keeping them away from me isn't gonna do it either." Ryan asked, "Okay so what should I do?" "I don't know!" Troy shouted. "But I'm gonna help you figure it out. I believe you're a good dude and I love you like a brother but if I find out you lied to me, I'm gonna fuck you up for real!" He looked Ryan in the eye and said, "No lies Bro. Never." Ryan said, "No lies. I didn't touch her. She was my friend." They hugged and when they separated, both their faces were streaked with new tears. Troy said, "I'm sorry I thought you were gay, Bro." Ryan said, "No worries, Bro. I get it. Thanks for bringing it to me though, instead of talking behind my back." Troy said, "Brothers don't do that."

Troy was at his desk when Misty called him back. She wasn't far away and wanted to know if he wanted to meet her for dinner. Of course, he did! He was really falling for her. "Who wouldn't?" He thought. She was beautiful inside and out. She was like one of those songs where the beautiful girl doesn't know she's beautiful. She was insecure about her looks. At first, he thought she was just acting that way, but as he got to know her, he realized that she really was shy. He didn't understand it, but he didn't need to. He was falling in love with her and that's all that mattered. He'd never met anyone like her. She was so caring and sensitive, but tough as nails when she needed to be. She had taken a self-defense class and one day she was showing him some of her new moves. He pushed her harder than intended and she tumbled. When he went to help her up, she caught him with a shin sweep, and he went down like a ton of bricks. She laughed and jabbed at him mockingly. He grabbed her and kissed her passionately. They made love for the first time that night. She seemed apprehensive at first, but then she gave in to his kisses. Troy had been with plenty of women, but the emotion he felt from Misty that night was like nothing he'd felt before. There was a hunger that was almost primal. He tried to remove her shirt, but she stopped him. She backed up and removed it herself. She looked him in the eyes as she did it. She removed all her clothes and stood naked before him. Her body was covered with scars. Now he understood why she was so shy. "What happened to you?" he asked. "Was it…" Misty stopped him. "One day I'll tell you." She kissed him. She gave herself to him that night. He was so gentle. When her body exploded in orgasm she cried. It was everything she imagined her first time would be and so much more. She loved this man, and he loved her.

A phone ringing brought him back to the present. He realized it was his phone and answered it. "Roman here." He answered. "What up kid?" Ryan said. "Hey scrub." Troy said as they both started laughing. Ryan asked, "So what do you want to eat tonight?" Troy slapped himself on the head. He'd forgotten that he made plans with Ryan, but he wouldn't, no couldn't cancel on Misty. Then it occurred to him. "Hey um, how would you feel if we have a third?" He asked Ryan. Ryan said, "Let me guess, Misty? You double booked, didn't you?" His silence was all the answer he needed. "Come on Bro? Troy begged. "I want you to meet her, anyway. Ryan laughed and said, "Okay! Okay! But I'm not bringing a date. When I'm ready to go I'm out. I don't need them becoming besties and I have to stay all night. Or worse they hate each other. Then the entire night will be awkward." Troy started to protest but stopped himself. Ryan was in and he knew he'd get along with Misty. His two favorite people were finally going to meet each other. He sat back and smiled. "See you later

Bro!" he said as he hung up the phone and got back to work.

"Yes, Mama yes!!" Renee shouted when Misty stepped into the living room. "You like?" Misty said as she twirled past them. "Troy is introducing me to his best friend tonight." "And when do we get to meet him?" Goldie asked. "Soon, soon!" Misty said waving her hands. "I told you I have to make sure he's the one before I bring him into this crazy family. Tonight, I'll get closer to an answer. You can tell a lot about a person by the company they keep." She bumped Renee with her hip. They all laughed.

Troy arrived at the restaurant early. He flashed his badge to get a better table and had a drink to steady his nerves. He couldn't believe he was this nervous. His best friend. His brother was meeting the woman he loved. There were so many things that could go wrong. They could hate each other or worse, they could already know each other. "Get a grip, kid." He said to himself. "It's gonna go how it's gonna go. The train has left the station." He finished his drink and waited for them to arrive. When Ryan got to the restaurant, Troy was on his second drink. He sat down and joined him, and they waited for Misty. When Misty walked in and saw Ryan sitting with Troy, she froze. They hadn't noticed her yet, and she considered leaving. Instead, she ran into the bathroom. "How could this be?" she said to herself. Ryan was Troy's best friend? Her Ryan? "Did all murder sprees go this crazy? Probably! That's why they all got caught." She said to her reflection. She had to decide what to do. Stay and have dinner with the person who caused her so much pain. The person who led her into the woods to be attacked. The person she planned to kill or leave and make up an excuse to give Troy and her family. Yes, her plan required meeting with Ryan, but she planned on meeting him as someone else. And what would she do about Troy? How could such a great guy be friends with Ryan? She wanted to cry at the thought of breaking up with him, but she didn't have a choice. The mission came first. It's all that mattered. She had been toying with the idea of leaving New York when her mission was complete, but meeting Troy had changed things. Now she knew she'd have to leave. Tears formed in her eyes again. She shook her head and cleared her thoughts. She could do this, she had to. Yes, it was unexpected, but she could make it work. She hadn't approached Ryan yet, so this was it. She straightened her clothes, checked her makeup, and walked out of the bathroom. She walked slowly to the table, trying to look happy. Troy saw her and stood up. "Here she is!" he said. Ryan stood up too. He was so handsome. She looked at Troy and smiled. "Hey you!" He gave her a tight hug and kissed her gently. "This is Ryan. Ryan, this is Misty." he said. Ryan reached out his hand and said, "it's nice to meet you, Misty!" "Now I see why my boy is so crazy about you". He nudged Troy and said, "You did good Bro!" They laughed and Misty tried to join in. "You okay?" Troy asked, looking concerned. "Yeah, I'm okay, lunch is sticking with me a little longer than usual." She gave an embarrassed giggle. "I know the feeling." Ryan said. "Let me find out you were nervous about tonight." Troy said jokingly. Misty sat down. She looked at Ryan. He looked so pleasant and so friendly. She knew the truth, though. There was a monster inside. She looked into his eyes and wondered would she be able to kill this man. Yes, she could kill. She'd done it once, but now Troy complicated things. Was he a monster, too? She looked at Troy. He placed his hand on hers and said, "Don't be nervous, babe." She gave him a weak smile. "How long have you been friends?" She asked Ryan and Troy. "Let the show begin." She thought to herself. They told her their story. She listened, collecting info to use later. She was also dissecting everything for a sign that Troy was a monster in hiding, too. Ryan was charming and single. She wondered why. By any list, he was a good catch. He had a sadness to him, though. It was just behind his smiling eyes. Most people wouldn't see it. Maybe she could because she'd seen it before. Every time she looked in the mirror, it was there. She'd been waiting for it to go away. She had a new face and life, but it was still there. She wondered if he saw it in her eyes, too. Misty listened to their stories and laughed in all the right places. It wasn't all fake. Ryan was charming. He was a lot like she pictured adult Ryan to be. She could tell he loved Troy. There was a level of hero worship there too. She wondered what Troy had done to deserve that. Maybe he protected him from bullies or got him out of a bad situation. A situation that would be career ending for an attorney. "So, Troy told me you grew up in the foster care system." Ryan said. "Yes, and he told me you work with foster kids." Misty replied. "Yes!" He replied. "I think it's very important that they have proper guidance from someone that cares and isn't just there to get paid." "That is very noble of you!" Misty said. "Positive role models are definitely in short supply in the system." "Exactly!" He replied. "We always tell our kids that they have to choose wisely when it comes to the people they decide to be around. I know it doesn't seem like those choices are theirs, but they are, to a degree. You can be placed with a family or in a facility with good people or bad people. It's important to learn the difference and set your own values based on the type of person you want to be. I tell them that if a person's values don't align with yours doesn't mean you can't get along with them. We all interact cordially with people we wouldn't be friends with all the time. That's life! But you don't follow those people. Especially if they're trying to get you to go along with things you know are wrong. That's where knowing who you are and having your own values and morals comes in. You don't want to spend your life paying for something you did as a kid." He trailed off and just stared at his plate. Missy stared at him. Was he talking about that night? She wondered. Troy broke the silence. Well, that took an unnecessarily serious turn. "He gets so caught up with those kids." He said a little awkwardly. "I'm sorry." Ryan giggled uncomfortably. He raised his glass. "To the kids!" They repeated and toasted "to the kids! "Where did you grow up, Ryan?" Misty asked. "Long Island." He replied. "Okay! I bet you were hell on wheels as a kid, too. You had to be just to keep up with this one." she said. She looked at Troy and smiled. He smiled too. He was happy they were getting along. "Hell on wheels? It's funny a girl I knew back then used to say that about me and my friends." Ryan said, looking at her. "Where did you grow up?" Misty choked on her drink. She knew she'd messed up as soon as she'd said it, but she hoped he hadn't caught it. "Ryan jumped in and said, man everybody says that. Plus, if you'd known Misty as a kid, I know you wouldn't have forgotten such a pretty face." "True." Ryan said laughing a bit. Troy raised his glass to toast again. "To memory lane!" "To memory lane." Ryan and

Misty repeated. Misty excused herself and went to the lady's room. She splashed some cold water on her neck and took some deep breaths. Why had she said that? She almost gave it up. Well, he would never recognize her face, but maybe her voice saying certain words or phrases. She had to be more careful. When she got back to the table, they were discussing Paul's murder case. "Time to go!" she said to herself. She sat down and awkwardly reached for her drink and spilled it all over the table and herself. Ryan and Troy both jumped in to minimize the mess, but it was too late. Troy helped her pat her clothes dry, but the dinner was clearly over. "Well, I guess that's that." Troy said, laughing. "I can't have my lady walking around looking like she just stabbed someone." They all laughed. "I have to prep for a meeting tomorrow anyway." Ryan said. "It was nice meeting you Misty. Hopefully you'll stick around, and we'll do this again." Misty giggled uncomfortably, and said, "minus the carnage. I'm sorry." Pointing at her dress. Ryan said, "No worries." In the Uber she apologized for the 100th time. "Babe, it's okay!" Troy said as he kissed her forehead again and again. She loved it when he did that. She felt so secure with him. Was this love? Was she in love with Ryan's best friend?

Ryan got home, showered, and sat in his favorite chair. He couldn't get Misty off his mind. She was beautiful and quirky. He giggled. But there was something else, something familiar and sad. Maybe the sadness was it, but he felt like he'd seen those eyes before. "Or maybe you got a crush on your boy's girl, dummy." He said to himself. Whatever it was he had to leave it at the door because he would definitely have to see her again and he couldn't let a girl come between him and Troy. He dreamed about Misty that night. They were all at the table having dinner, then he was running through the woods again. He woke up sweating and crying. He really didn't want to see Missy again. She had a weird effect on him, and he wasn't sure he would be able to hide it.

8

The next morning, Misty took a long walk. This week had been absolutely madness. First, she discovers Kevin is a member of the club she worked at. She absolutely could not use her anti-CSI kit at his murder, but she probably wouldn't need to. The minute the cops saw his equipment, they wouldn't investigate too much. She assumed he had whips and chains and things at home. Unless they connected him to the first murder, but that was unlikely. She thanked her lucky stars again for not using anything from that club in her anti-CSI kit. And then there was dinner. "What the entire fuck?!" she said a little too loud. A lady walking past her looked around to see what Misty was referring to. "It's nothing I thought I saw something." Mitsy said awkwardly. The lady rolled her eyes, "fucking tourists" she mumbled. First,

Troy approaches her right after she commits her first murder and now, he's best friends with Ryan, whom she plans to murder. "Who was this guy?" She thought again for the millionth time, "is this a setup?" Could this all be a coincidence? If it was a setup, she'd have been arrested by now. Coincidence then, but damn, this was the mother of all coincidences. "Oh well, the mission must be completed." She said to herself. "I have to break up with Troy. Or I can stay with him. That way I can keep tabs on the cases and Ryan." Maybe this was a good thing. She still didn't want to pray for good fortune on a murder spree, but it seemed like the universe was on her side.

Later that week, Misty had another date with Kevin. They went out to eat, walked around a little and then he asked her to come back to his place. When they got there, another man was waiting for them. Kevin introduced him as Germaine, a friend visiting from out of town. Misty tried to leave, but they insisted she stay. She said she'd stay for one drink. Germaine made the drinks. He was very charming. The conversation was going well, and the night was flowing along. Misty thought about staying a little longer until she felt a little off. She recognized the feeling immediately. They had drugged her. Her recon on Kevin had been helpful, but it had not been complete. She had seen no sign that Kevin was into drugging and torturing women. Yes, he liked to go to the club, but a lot of people did and that's where their fetish stopped. Apparently, Kevin's did not. Misty knew exactly what drug they had given her because she had been drugged before. "Oh no!" she thought and began to panic. How could this be happening? Kevin was as good at hiding his true nature as she was. She couldn't let this happen. The first time she was a trusting kid, now she was, "was what?" She thought. She wasn't sure what she was, but she knew what she wasn't. She wasn't a victim. Not anymore. "Okay get it together." She told herself. "You trained for this get up!" Saying this to herself, she rose from the couch. "Where are you going, doll?" Germaine asked. "Gotta tinkle." She said with a little girly gesture. "Ain't she the cutest?" Germaine asked Kevin. Misty thought maybe she didn't miss anything. Maybe this was all Germaine's doing. It didn't really matter though it. This was happening.

While conducting her research on how to be a competent killer, Misty came across a lot of files where victims were drugged. She wasn't planning on being the victim, but she didn't think that anybody did. She lived in New York City and although she didn't feel like it, she was a very attractive woman, and she was going on a murder spree. Those three things, especially that last one, increased her chances of being a victim. That's when she enrolled in a self-defense class and decided to drug herself. She had gotten ahold of the most used date drugs and under very controlled and private settings, she drugged herself until she was an expert on the effects each one had on her body and mind. So, when she started to lose feeling in her cheeks, she knew exactly what they had given her. It was the same drug she planned on using on Kevin at first. As she excused herself and went to the bathroom, she played the drugged girl part. She had this act down pack. She knew how long she had before she'd be as limp as a rag doll. She knew she had to act fast. She bumped into the walls and stumbled a bit, even inside the bathroom. Her thoughts were getting a little foggy. She had maybe 30 minutes before she'd be unable to move. She felt around in her bag and found the injections she had packed in her glasses case. She only needed one, but she brought two just in case. She went back into the living room with each syringe tucked into her sleeve. "Here she comes!" Said Kevin. "You ready to party?" He asked Germaine. "Yes, I am!" Germaine answered as he guided Misty to the couch and sat her down between them. They started rubbing their hands along her legs and breasts. She pretended to return their affections. When she ran her hands across their shoulders, she injected them both in the neck. "What the fuck? What did you do? What was that?" They were both hurling questions at her as they jumped up. "I thought you guys wanted the party." she said. Her words slurred a bit. Kevin tried to say something as he fell to the floor. The drugs she used were fast acting. She couldn't take the chance that her victim would overpower her in the seconds or minutes that it took for the drugs to kick in. People tend to be angry after being injected against their will. She giggled at this thought. Now that the guys were out, she sat back on the couch and let the effects take hold. The drug they'd given her was a paralytic that left you fully aware but unable to move. She had eaten a healthy meal and only had a couple glasses of wine, so she figured she wouldn't be down for too long. She laid there for what felt like an eternity. She prayed this time, that the drug she had given them would work as planned. If they woke up before she was able to move, they would kill her. They'd do a lot more than that but ultimately, they would kill her. She went over the plan again and scolded herself for not seeing this coming, for ending up this way. She shouldn't have been surprised though, remembering what he did to her. "Nope, nope, not now." She stopped the memory. She could not afford this right now. She had to be ready. As soon as she was able to move, she had to get going. She rearranged her plan to include one more. "Now this is going to be good!" She thought. She felt a faint smile creep across her face and was overjoyed! The drug was wearing off. Over 4 hours had passed and now she was in control of her body again. Kevin and Germaine were still unconscious. She tied them up and went in search of Kevin's toys.

When Kevin woke up, he didn't know where he was. It was dark and he couldn't move. He looked around and thought, "Okay, so I'm home, but why can't I move?" He closed his eyes and tried to remember what had happened. "Oh shit!" He said out loud. "Kevin?" Germaine said. "What happened?" He asked. "That bitch drugged us!" Kevin answered. "Yes, I did." Misty said. "But in all fairness, you drugged me first." she said. Both men started yelling "Bitch you better let us go! I'll kill you bitch!" "Yeah, yeah, yeah." Misty giggled. They yelled and cursed for a few more minutes. When they stopped, Misty spoke. "Are you done?" The men nodded. "Let me tell you a story. It's about a group of boys that beat and raped a girl." Kevin's eyes widened. "Years later, that girl decides to take revenge on those boys. She plots and plans." "No, no." Kevin interrupted. "It can't be, it can't be." Misty continued. "She's at his place to kill him and he and his friend," she points to Germaine who is crying, "drug her. What are the odds?" "We didn't drug you." Germain said. Kevin was just staring at her. How could this be? Nobody had seen her or heard from her in years. "Don't lie to me. I know exactly what you gave me. I didn't see that coming, but I was prepared, so hey!" She threw up her hands. All her doubts were gone. "This was just for me, but now that I know you didn't stop, that you kept attacking women and even found a new accomplice, it's for all your victims too." "No, no. We didn't. I didn't." Germaine was saying, "Help! Help!" He screamed. "Stop!" Kevin shouted. "You know nobody is going to hear you." He turned to Misty. "You can't be her. I don't know who you are, but you can't be her. You better let us go before this goes too far." He struggled against his restraints. "I know people! People that will find you!" He was yelling now. Missy just sat there, looking at him. "Yes, Kevin, I am her." "You..." he tried to interrupt her. "No." She held up her hand and stopped him from talking. "I thought you destroyed me. But you didn't. I'm sure you thought you did. Is that why you do this?" She asked, pointing at his equipment." Do you get off on destroying people? You are a piece of shit Kevin." She said through gritted teeth. She sat there for a moment, then she spoke again. "Well, I guess we should get to it." The men were trying to speak but could only manage grumbles. "Oh yeah,

I drugged you again. You won't pass out this time, though. Germaine you really picked the wrong night to visit." While they were passed out, she assembled Kevin's swing and secured Germaine in its straps. She hoisted Germaine up. He began flailing, but he didn't have much wiggle room. There was a loop around his neck and one under his arms. "And for you." Misty said as she approached Kevin. "You like to watch." She turned his chair to face Germaine. He tried to fight and head-butted her. "Ow! she said, jumping back. I should just kill you now, but no, that'll be too good for you. You need to suffer. Suffer like all the women you've hurt or killed. Did you kill them like you tried to kill me?" She was screaming now. For the first time, Kevin looked genuinely frightened. She walked over to Germaine and released the hook under his arms. He immediately began to choke. Missy left the room. She couldn't watch this man die. When she returned, he was dead, and Kevin was crying. "Really?" She asked. "You cry for him? Or is it more for yourself?" She unzipped his pants and removed his penis. She began massaging it. When he got aroused, she removed his hand from his binds, placed it around his penis and continued to stroke. His grunts of protest became moans of pleasure. He climaxed, spraying semen all over himself and the floor. Misty had thought about collecting semen from the club, but she knew fresh was best. She hated the thought of him having any pleasure at her expense, but it was for the mission. After she was done, she began cleaning. He watched her with amazement as she sprayed and wiped down anything that would have any trace of her on it. For a moment, Kevin let himself believe she wasn't going to kill him. That she was framing him for killing Germaine. But as it became harder for him to breathe, that fantasy faded. He would be found like this, and everyone would know. He looked up at Germaine's dead body and said, "and you wanted to install cameras. Good thing I didn't do that shit! Women are going come forward and tell what we did to them but there won't be any proof." Then the thought occurred to him. "If she really is her, did she kill Paul?" This scared him the most. "How could this be happening? I have to warn the guys! I can't warn anybody. Am I really going to die like this?" he thought. As his breaths got harder to come by, he prayed. "God I'm sorry.

I don't know why I'm this way or why I'm surprised that is ending this way." Misty finished cleaning. When she returned to the living room, Kevin had stopped breathing, "Good!" She thought. She couldn't watch him die either, she gathered her things and left after doing one last walkthrough. She'd used all his cleaning products so the only thing she had to throw out were her gloves. She didn't think he had cameras because he had done a piece on them, and he was strictly against them being inside his home, but she checked anyway. When she was satisfied, she left.

Misty left Kevin's building looking like a different person. This time she exited as a man. A short wig, baggy clothes, and a swagger that she copied from a man she followed one day. She had her disguise from earlier in a backpack. His building had cameras, but the hat she wore covered her face just in case the cops checked it, but she didn't think they would. She said a prayer as she walked to the subway. "Thank you, Lord, for protecting me! I know I don't make it easy, but I am truly thankful! Amen!" She had planned on taking the subway home, but now she just walked and walked and walked. It was cold, but she barely noticed. She was pissed, at herself for almost becoming the victim. It didn't matter if it was Kevin or Germaine that had drugged her. She'd done research on Kevin. She thought she was thorough in her research, but she wasn't. It was sloppy and it almost cost her everything. And then there was Troy and Ryan. Friends. Best friends. She had never thought to check out their friends. How was she going to continue to be with Troy after she killed his best friend? What if she messed up again, and he caught her? She had to come up with a new plan. There was no way she could have planned for all this. "God, thank you for getting me out of there!" She prayed again. She still didn't feel comfortable praying for a successful killing spree, but she could ask for protection. That night Misty lay in bed, unable to sleep. She had killed someone that wasn't on her list. Yes, he was about to harm her, but was it self-defense? She could have killed Kevin and left a Germaine alive. "And then what?" She asked herself. "Let him go and hope he wouldn't tell the cops?" That may have worked. He would have to admit his part in drugging her. "Yeah, right, he'd leave that part out for sure." She sighed. What's done is done. No, he hadn't done anything to her yet, but he would have if given the chance. He was a monster, just like Kevin. Who knows how many women they'd hurt? They'd planned to hurt someone tonight. They just picked the wrong someone. She saved herself tonight and countless other women.

9

The next week was quiet. Misty worked on a few designs and tried her best to have a few normal days. Kevin and Germaine's bodies had been found, and the police had released the video of them with a person who appeared to be a woman entering the building. The details had not been made public, but an anonymous source said that there was a sexual theme to the scene. Troy hadn't mentioned it to her, so maybe he didn't know Kevin. It was possible that Ryan hadn't kept in touch with him. She really liked this guy. Maybe he was the good guy she'd prayed for. The timing was horrible but what was she going to do. She knew she might have to leave New York and never see him again so she had to make as many good memories as possible. She decided it was time for Troy to meet her family. When she told Goldie that she wanted them to meet him, she was elated. "So, this is real, huh?" Goldie asked.

Misty blushed. "Yeah, I think so. He introduced me to his best friend so I should introduce him to you, my family. Do you want to meet him alone or should we include the guys? If we don't invite them, we'll never hear the end of it." Goldie said, "You're right!" Misty said. "Now, are you sure he's going to be okay with?" Goldie pointed to herself. "He'd better be, or he's not the one for me." Misty said. "That's my girl!" Goldie said, pinching Misty's cheek. "Let me know what day works for you, and I'll make sure the boys are present and prepped." Goldie said.

While Misty was planning her introductory dinner, she was also planning her next murder. Sean was next. She had followed him a few times, but she hadn't spoken to him. She was still trying to figure out how to approach him. His IG wasn't any help. He didn't post much. She needed to step it up if she was going to get next to him. That evening, Misty went for a walk. All the planning had her mentally exhausted. Thinking so much about Sean had taken her thoughts back to her childhood. He was so mean to her. He would make fun of her every chance he got. He'd say she was stupid, and that's why she hadn't been adopted. Nobody wanted a stupid kid. Bullies were a part of life for a lot of kids, not just foster kids. She knew she hadn't had the worst childhood, especially after talking to some of the girls at the club. But it still hurt, to think about it. Then there was that night that they attacked her. She often wondered what her life would have been like if it hadn't happened. Would she have gotten married and had kids, or been single and sassy? "Instead of a surgically engineered introvert on a killing spree." She laughed out loud. "Don't forget crazy!" She mumbled to herself. Over the years, she'd had ups and downs. A lot of downs, but God had blessed her with love and a family that she couldn't get rid of if she tried. She loved her life, and she wanted to live it to the fullest. That's why she had to complete the mission. She toyed with the idea of stopping and just being happy with getting half of them, but she knew killing them all was the only way to stop the pain that the hatred and hurt still caused. She couldn't move on until they were all gone. Misty realized that her old methods wouldn't work. She couldn't risk trying to date him now that she'd met Ryan. What if they were still friends and Sean showed him a picture of her? She followed him home one evening and saw there was a young doorman that greeted him. "Could that work?" She asked herself. Could she get close to doorman and gain access to Sean's apartment that way? She still needed a disguise but that really could work. She went back the next day pretending to be a dog walker offering her services. His name was Reggie, and he was very happy to meet her. He lived in Brooklyn and only came into the city for work. He was perfect.

The news about Kevin's deaths hit way harder than Misty had expected. As it turned out Germaine was famous. The story had been rather quiet until the media found out he was with Kevin. Germaine's publicist tried to keep it a secret, but it didn't work for long. When the news broke about who he really was and how they died, the story took on a life of its own. Misty worried about the video of her walking in with them. "They'll be looking even harder for me now. They probably have private detectives now. Maybe even the FBI!" she said to the empty room. She collapsed onto the bed, breathing hard. "How could this be? What should I do? This is officially the worst murder spree ever!" She took a few deep breaths and calmed herself down. "Okay girl, get a grip. Yes, this is a mess, but let's regroup and see where we actually are." She said to herself. "Will there be people looking for you? Correction looking for the mystery woman?" She put in air quotes. "Yes, but nobody knows who she is or how she left the building." Check! She checked an imaginary box in the win column. "More detectives mean extra scrutiny." She checked the box in the get caught column. She was sure she hadn't left any traces of herself but wasn't everybody. "Yeah, right, until they got caught because of a drop of spit or an eyelash. Did that really happen, or was that in a movie?" She asked herself. "It doesn't matter." she said, shaking her head. "It's not like I can go back and change anything." All she could do was use her relationship with Troy to keep tabs on the investigation. Now that there was a celebrity involved, he wouldn't or shouldn't think her curiosity was weird or suspicious. The video was all over the Internet and so far, nobody had asked if she looked familiar. She practically stopped breathing when the video came on the news when she was watching TV with Goldie and the twins. They had a lot to say, but nothing about recognizing her. They wished they knew who she was so they could get the reward money. Well, that's how Renee felt. Ralph thought they deserved what they got. Especially since they had probably killed her and disposed of the body. "You know rich people got cleaners and shit. They come through and get rid of all the evidence like poof!" He said waving his hands like a magician. "Is that how they do it?" Goldie asked "Poof?" They all laughed. Even Misty joined in. She loved these people so much! She had to make sure she didn't get caught. She couldn't bear to lose them, to lose this. She couldn't imagine life without them. She really didn't have to imagine it. She'd already experienced it. She also couldn't bear the thought of them knowing what she'd done. Would they understand, or would they think she was the monster?

Misty's phone buzzed. It was Reggie, confirming their date. She was meeting him at his job, and they were going to dinner. It was her idea to meet him at work. She told him she'd be in the area, plus she enjoyed seeing him in his uniform.

"Hey uniform groupies are a thing." She told herself. Of course, the real reason was that she needed to do some recon on the layout of the building and its security system. Getting the info was easier than she thought. Reggie was all too happy to explain everything. She asked questions and said, "wow they really trust you with all this? These apartments must cost a fortune!" Her groupie act worked perfectly. He was so proud when he showed her his master key. "This right here gets me into every apartment in the building. They run background checks on all the guys, but some residents still don't allow entry if they don't like you. You know? But me? I got this because they all approved me! It's a two key system and the other keys are kept in there." He pointed out the lockbox on the wall. "Two keys?" she asked. "Yeah." he said. "They all have the key to their individual lock and this one he held up the master key." "Okay, I get it. You have the master and access to these so you can enter anytime they need you to." Misty said. "Exactly!" Reggie beamed. No one had ever been curious about his work except other guys looking for work. Now this beautiful woman was asking questions and loving it. She understood how important he was around here. He knew it would happen one day. Misty saw how proud he was and almost felt bad for deceiving him. She'd make sure he didn't get blamed for anything. He really was a good guy. Their went well. If she wasn't already dating Troy, she'd considered making this a real thing. It was going to be hard to dump him later. Maybe she wouldn't have to. If this all went to plan, he'd never know it was her and nobody would know the killer had gained access because of him. Yeah, Troy was great, but nothing was promised, and alternate plans were never a bad thing.

10

Today was the day! The day that Misty had been looking forward to and dreading at the same time. Troy was going to meet Goldie and the twins tonight at dinner. They had chosen to have dinner at their apartment. Goldie cooked while Misty, Ralph and Renee cleaned and set the table. "Why are you so quiet, sis?" Renee asked. Misty had been very quiet tonight. She didn't even respond to their jokes about her not being able to cook for her man. "You that nervous girl? It's gonna be fine! You watch! He's gonna love us! I mean, who doesn't?" Misty smiled. "Yeah, you're right, but he's the first," she paused. "He's the first everything." she said as she plopped down on the couch. Goldie came and sat next to her. "I know honey, it feels like everything is riding on this dinner going well. But it's not. We are admittedly not everyone's cup of tea and he's a cop. Most of them are straight laced know-it-alls but I don't think you would like him so much or at all, for that matter, if he was like that. I trust your instincts. If all goes well, that's great! If we don't like him or he doesn't like us, it's okay. As long as everybody can agree to disagree, we'll live to eat another day." "But how can I date a guy that doesn't like my family?" Misty asked. "I don't know, baby. That's something you'll have to figure out for yourself." Goldie said. "Just remember, there's a big difference between dislike and disrespect."

Ryan was at his desk reading the stories about Kevin's death. They were mostly about the other guy, Germaine, but some of the local news stories spoke a little more about Kevin. He'd watched the video dozens of times, hoping to see something familiar about the woman they were with. "Could it be her? Or maybe someone she sent?" He asked his laptop. If it wasn't her, it was one hell of a coincidence. Paul then Kevin. It seemed like Kevin was into some kinky shit, so it could be a coincidence. One article said he was a member of one of those dominatrix sex clubs where they had all types of torture devices. "Are you really surprised? The whole thing had been his idea." Ryan said to his laptop again. He decided he should reach out to the only other guy that was there that night. He didn't want to. He had been an asshole back then, and he doubted if he'd changed, other than maybe being a bigger asshole now. He Google Sean Crissler and was surprised to see that he didn't have much of a social media presence. He had thought he would have had multiple accounts showing off his sexual conquests, fast cars, and lavish lifestyle. His socials didn't give any real clues to what he was up to these days. He looked up his LinkedIn account and was able to find out where Sean worked. He was a project manager for a cybersecurity firm. Ryan called the firm and was transferred to Sean. "Crissler!" Sean answered. "Hey Sean. This is Ryan. Ryan Breaker." "I've been expecting your call." Sean said. "We should talk in person. Don't you think?" "Yeah, I guess." Ryan answered. They arranged to meet at a restaurant in midtown for lunch.

They both got there early. They sat down, ordered drinks, and secretly hoped the situation wasn't what they thought it was. "It's been a while." Sean said sipping his drink. "Yeah, it has." Ryan replied. "You look good. Doing well for yourself." "Likewise! You're an attorney, right?" Sean asked. "So, we've both done our homework." Ryan thought to himself. "Yeah, I work with youth offenders, mostly. I try to catch them before they do something that will ruin their lives." They both just stared at each other for a moment. "I get it." Sean said. "So, you think the deaths are related? You think it's because of what we did?" "It's possible. I mean, things happen, but." Ryan trailed off. Sean said. "Yeah but? Has anyone contacted you about it? I haven't spoken to either of them in years." He said, referring to Paul and Kevin. Have you spoken to them lately? "No. I haven't spoken to any of you since that last time." Ryan replied. The last time he had spoken to any of them was right after graduation. He was still coping with what they had done, and seeing them go on like nothing had happened was infuriating. He told them not to speak to him ever again. That they were evil, and they would all be punished for what they had done. He said he would spend his life searching for her and doing everything he could to make up for what they'd done. He said he wished he'd never met any of them and he meant it, then and now. Sean sighed and said, "Look man, I get it. I didn't then. None of us did. We were just happy we didn't go to jail. Were you ever able to find her?" "No." Ryan replied. "Maybe that's a good thing." Sean said. "I mean, what would you have said? Would she even want to hear anything you had to say? She probably ran off and started tricking in another city somewhere." Brian shot a disgusted look at Sean. "Are you serious? She wasn't a prostitute." Sean raised his hands and said, "Hey that's what everybody said after she disappeared." "Yeah, cause Paul made it up!" Ryan yelled. He looked around and saw that some of the people at the restaurant were stating at them. He lowered his voice and said, "I knew meeting with you was a bad idea. You didn't care then, and you don't now. You've convinced yourself that the lies we told were real." "Wait man wait." Sean said when Ryan got up to leave. "I'm sorry. I couldn't allow myself to live in that moment forever. So yes, I've forgotten some of the details. We were kids! We fucked up, but why should we have to live in it for the rest of our lives?" Sean said. "Why should we have to live with it? What about her? Do you think she was able to forget it and move on?" Ryan said, standing up again. "Look out for yourself, man. Just in case." Ryan said as he got up and threw a $20 bill on the table. Sean watched him walk away. "What if it is related?" He said to himself. "Whatever." He shrugged it off. He lived in a secure building and had very little interaction with the public at work. His world was a neat little bubble that he controlled, and he wasn't going to allow any new people in until things felt different. He hadn't admitted to himself until now that something had felt off since he heard about Paul's death. He thought it was just how people felt when a childhood friend died, but now he wasn't so sure. He shrugged off the thought. How could it be her that killed them? A woman was able to kill three men. Two at a time in Kevin's case? No, that couldn't be her in the video. "What was she some sort of trained assassin? What if it is though?" His brain shouted back. "I guess we'll find out, won't we? She'll either come for us or she won't. What's done is done and no one can change it."

Misty met Troy at his job. She wanted to tell him about Goldie and the Twins before he met them. If she got the faintest whiff of indifference, she was going to call it off. They stopped at a bench and sat down. "What's going on?" Troy asked her. "You look so serious." "I need to tell you some things about my family. Goldie, my mom, is a trans woman, and the twins aren't really twins. Their friends who became family and they're gay. Like over the top Nathan Lane in The Birdcage, gay. And I love them all more than any person could possibly love anyone!" She looked him in the eyes, looking for a reaction. "Okay!" He said, "Can she cook?" He smiled. Misty burst into laughter. "Really, is that your only question?" She asked him. She was laughing so hard now that tears were welling up in her eyes. She hugged him and said a silent prayer, "thank you God for this wonderful man." She told him how she'd met her family while they walked. He noticed how similar their lives were. Finding friends that became family. He wasn't surprised when she told him how she had come to Goldie's aide. She was one of the strongest people he'd ever met. The conversation turned to him and Ryan. She could feel how much he loved him and thought again about how his death would affect him. He would probably turn to her for comfort. "Damn, that sounds next level evil." She said to herself. The murderer comforting the loved ones of her victim. "Damn." By the time they got to the apartment building, Misty had given Troy the full story of how her family had become a family. He had asked questions, but they were normal questions for this type of situation. She thought so anyway. She'd never been in this situation before. "Am I in a real relationship? With a real man? Is this real?" She asked herself. She bit the inside of her jaw as a reality check. Yep, it hurt, and he was still there beside her, so she decided that it was indeed real. She giggled and Troy asked, "what's so funny?" "This" she said. "You're about to meet my family at a family dinner. It's like we're on a TV show." He smiled and asked, "what would the name of this show be?" "The cop and the crazies!" she replied. They broke out into laughter. They were laughing so loud and when they got to the door, that Goldie opened it before Misty had a chance to pull out her keys. "I'll take this as a good sign!" Goldie said as they walked in. It took a few minutes for them to stop laughing, but it was a perfect entrance. Their laughter was infectious and the joy that was on Misty's face was all her family needed to see. When they stopped laughing, Misty looked up and saw the smiles on everyone's faces and knew that the evening would go well. "Guys, this is Troy. Troy, this is my mom, Goldie." Troy reached out and took Goldie's hand. "Hello ma'am. It's a pleasure to meet you!" "Likewise! Anybody that makes her smile like that is welcome in my home!" Goldie said. "These two are Ralph and Renee." Misty said, blushing now. "Pleasure to meet you." Troy said, shaking hands with the guys. "Oh, honey, the pleasure is all ours!" Renee said. Ralph slapped his hand away as he tried to get another handshake from Troy. They all burst into laughter. This was already off to a great start. They talked and ate and talked some more. They talked and drank, late into the night. Troy couldn't remember ever being this comfortable around people he'd just met. He already loved Misty and now he was falling in love with her family. He looked over at her and marveled at how, in such a short time, she had brought so much joy into his life. Before he met Misty, his life was all about work and volunteering. Yeah, he had Ryan, but he didn't have this. He wasn't sure he even knew this existed. He was raised by his dad and didn't know much about his family. His mom was a drug addict and died young. He thought about looking his family up when he became a cop but decided against it. His life was good, and he was doing good by mentoring his kids, so why bring unnecessary emotional drama into his life? Now he thought it might be worth looking into if this was what family could be. They said their goodbyes around 1:00 AM. Troy left after kissing Misty goodnight and avoiding kisses from Renee. As he got into his Uber, he laughed out loud. He couldn't wait to tell Ryan about the dinner. "He's gonna love them!" He said to himself.

The next day, Misty was on cloud nine. Dinner had gone so well. Everybody loved everybody and she was overjoyed. "Alright time to get back to business girl." she told herself. The more she thought about how she was going to take care of Sean the more she realized she didn't really want to get Reggie in trouble and if there was a way to do this without involving him or the building, she'd have to find it. Anything that took place at the building would involve him being questioned, and if they questioned him and dug into his life, they would certainly get around to her. She really needed a new plan, and she had to stop seeing Reggie. All her original plans had her revealing herself to them right before they died so they would know exactly why this was happening. But for this one, she may have to scrap that part. Sean was insulated from outsiders at work and at home. The only place he was open was on his commute. He took the subway to work every day at 7:00 AM. Misty wasn't sure she could pull off a public execution. So many things had already gone wrong in controlled environments. She didn't want to think of all the things that could go wrong on a subway. There were cameras and people and more people. Steps and people. Moving trains and rats. Ooh, she hated rats. And there were more people, most of them with cameras. She'd have to be smart about this. Just then, another story about Germaine and Kevin popped up. A woman had come forward and said that they drugged her and raped her. The reporter said more women were going to come forward soon. Misty felt a wave of anger and relief at the same time. Anger at them for doing that and relief because they wouldn't ever get to do it again. She'd stopped them. This story was a sign that she was on the right path. She'd stopped two predators. She doubted if they'd be looking too hard for her now. She thought about that night, and it came to her. She could use the needle ring to inject Sean with the poison. If she wore a disguise, it wouldn't matter if some amateur filmmaker caught a shot of her. They wouldn't be able to see what she'd done, anyway. "Well, he would probably yell or something when he felt it. That would cause people to pay more attention." She thought. But what if he didn't feel it? She imagined how it would go. She acted it out, moving around in her bedroom. People were always bumping into each other on the subway. Just the other day...she trailed off. "That's it!" She said out loud. She remembered a guy had spilled hot coffee on another guy and they almost got into a fight. "I can spill hot coffee on him and inject him with a needle at the same time. He'd focus on the burn and wouldn't realize he'd been stuck. And if anyone caught it on video, that's all they'd see." Her timing had to be perfect. Right as they were entering or exiting the train. People would be bunched together, and he probably wouldn't know who'd done it. If she used something that took some time to kick in, he would be in his office when it started working. That was it. Now she had to find a good disguise. She still had the needles she used on Kevin and Germaine. They say you should never use needles twice, but she didn't think it mattered in this case. She giggled.

It had been a few days since she'd spoken to Reggie. She texted him that her boyfriend had come back into her life, and she couldn't see him anymore. Then she chucked the phone into the Hudson River. She missed him. All this time she couldn't find a decent guy and now she had found two. Maybe it wasn't them but her. Had she been the problem? Maybe she was too afraid to let someone really get to know her. But that meant she didn't get to know them either. She changed since she'd killed Paul. She had finally taken control of her life by taking his. She felt confident in a way she never thought possible, and meeting Troy just added to it. She felt like her inside was beginning to match the outside. Misty settled on a disguise for her mission. She would be an old man for this one. Nobody would think twice about an elderly man spilling coffee on someone. If her crowded exit trick didn't work, and he did see who'd done it, chances were that he wouldn't make too much of a fuss. You'd have to be a real dick to yell at an old guy. She went to the station near his home and waited, pretending to read the paper. Old people still read the actual newspaper. When she saw him coming, she made her way down the steps, went through the turnstile, and waited near the bench. He always rode in the same train car. He walked past her, not looking up once. He never spoke to anyone. When the train came, she got in ahead of him. She held a coffee in one hand and held onto the pole with the other. He was standing right beside her. This was perfect. When this train pulled into the station and everyone that was getting off, she got the needle ready. The doors opened and everyone started inching their way out. She bumped into him and spilled the coffee on the top of his arm and stuck him with the needle. He yelled "What the Fuck?!" Then he saw that it was an elderly guy. "Sorry. Sorry." Misty said. "Yeah whatever." Sean said, pushing his way through the crowd. Misty got off the train and left the station. She walked around for a while, then she went into

Macy's. She looked around then she left. She took a cab back to Sean's neighborhood. She followed the same route she'd taken that morning back into Central Park and the old man disappeared.

Sean was annoyed as he made his way upstairs to his office. The coffee had burned and now his arm was stinging, he hoped he didn't have to go to the hospital. "Some of these places make the coffee way too hot." He said to himself. He was in the bathroom trying to wash the coffee off his shirt sleeve when he felt the first sharp pain in his chest. He thought it was gas until he felt the second one. The third was stronger. He grabbed his chest and tried to call out for help, but he was the only one there. Most of the staff worked from home. He collapsed on the bathroom floor. It was an hour before they found his body.

While she was walking through Central Park, Misty had a thought. The park had become her phone booth. Superman always changed identities in a phone booth, and she had changed in Central Park a few times now. She laughed out loud. She had dumped the old guy disguise, but she still had the ring in her bag. "Probably not the best idea to be walking around with the murder weapon with the DNA of two victims on it." She thought. She smashed it with a rock and threw it into a storm drain. "Gone forever under New York City." She said as it disappeared into the darkness. The park was so beautiful! Before it became her phone booth, she would come to the park and just walk around and marvel at the architecture. She would always say a prayer thanking God for the sacrifices that were made by the occupants of the black neighborhood that was displaced to build it. Seneca Village was a thriving middle class neighborhood where black people owned their property. They were displaced in 1857 to build Central Park. So many wrongs were done in the name of progress.

11

A few days later, Troy met Ryan at their favorite meeting place. It was a bar that wasn't frequented by many cops or lawyers. The people that worked there knew Troy was a cop and that he didn't want it advertised. He was just another guy that liked the atmosphere. "So, how'd it go with the family?" Ryan asked Troy. "Man, they were so cool! So much so that I've reconsidered contacting my dad's family." Ryan was visibly shocked. "What?! You said you'd never look them up. This must have been a religious experience." He laughed. Troy said, "No, not religious, but moving. To meet people that can be that open and receptive to a stranger, it was incredible. I see why Misty loves them so much!" "Well, they are her family." Ryan said. "Yeah, but not biological, though. Like us!" Troy responded. "Oh! I thought that she'd reconnected with her biological family." Ryan said. Troy filled him in on how they became a family and how the dinner had gone. "Wow! So Misty was a runaway?" "Yes, scared and alone in a strange place, but brave enough to help a stranger." Troy said. Ryan could see how much he loved Misty. He still couldn't let go of the feeling that he'd met her before. "How old was she?" He asked. "I don't know. She said it was about 10 years ago, so 14 or 15, I guess. Crazy right?" Troy said as he took a drink. "You know, sometimes I feel like she was sent here to save me too." "From what?" Ryan asked, looking genuinely puzzled. "From myself! You know how I used to be. I dated, but they weren't right." This is the only relationship I really have." He said pointing to himself and Ryan. Ryan nodded in agreement. "And now I have her and possibly her family. I can't wait for you to meet them. It is truly an experience!" He said laughing. They stayed at the bar for a few more hours. They talked about an upcoming basketball game their team had. One of their best players had gotten caught up in a gang sweep and wouldn't be allowed to play until his case was cleared. He wasn't in a gang, but his brother was and when the sweep happened, they took them both. Ryan had a meeting with the DA in the morning. He hoped they could get it cleared up quickly.

On his way home, Ryan kept thinking about the story Misty had told Troy about how she met Goldie. That was around the time she had gone missing. "Could it be her?" he wondered. He didn't remember exactly what she looked like, but she didn't look like Misty. There was something familiar about her, though. There was something in her eyes. "Give it up, dummy." he said to himself, shaking his head. It's probably just a crush. You got a crush on your boy's girl. It'll pass." After his night out with Troy, Ryan realized he didn't like the way he left things with Sean. He was still an asshole, but like it or not they were in this together. If there was a this. He texted him. Sean didn't reply to any of Ryan's texts. At first, he figured he was just pissed, but then he began to worry after a few days. He called his job and was transferred to a woman. "Nancy Wells, how my help you?" The woman answered. "Hi, I'm looking for Sean Crissler." Ryan replied. "May I ask who's calling?" My name is Ryan Breaker." "Are you a client?" Ms. Wells asked. "No, I'm an old friend from school. If he's busy, you can just let him know that I called." Ms. Wells cleared her throat. "I'm sorry. I won't be able to do that. Mr. Crissler is dead." Ryan felt like he'd been kicked in the gut. "Dead? How? When? I just saw him last week." He said with the little bit of air left in his lungs. "I'm so sorry to tell you like this." Ms. Wells was saying "he had a heart attack Tuesday morning. His body was found around 11:00 AM." Ryan was silent. "Sir, are you there?" Ms. Wells asked. "Yes. I can't believe this. You're sure it was him? This isn't a joke or something. No sir I assure you this is not a joke. It was him." Ryan heard her sniffle a bit. "Thank you, thank you." he said as he hung up the phone. "Heart attack my ass!" He said to the empty room. "It was her and that means I'm next." What could he do to avoid it, though? She clearly had a plan and a good one. What was he going to do? Stay in the house forever? Leave the city? This was crazy!

Ryan called Troy. "Yeah, we gotta talk ASAP!" He said into the phone. "What's going on? You sound crazy!" Troy replied. "I hope I am. How fast can you get here?" Ryan asked. "Give me

20 minutes." Troy replied, sensing the frantic tone and Ryan's voice. He got to Ryan's place as fast as he could. Once he was in the apartment, he searched for intruders, thinking that Ryan had been robbed or something. "What's up?" He said, breathing hard. "Sit down. I have something to tell you." Ryan said. They sat down at the kitchen table and Ryan told Troy he thought the murders were connected and how. When he was done Troy was speechless for a long moment. "Why didn't you say something earlier?" Troy asked. "Man, I didn't know for sure. There was the gay thing with Paul and Kevin's story." he said, exasperated. "It could have been a coincidence, but now Sean. They're connected and I'm next. I'm the only one left!" He said as he started to cry. Troy lowered his head. He didn't have the words to comfort Ryan. After what seemed like forever, Troy spoke. "Okay. If this is what it seems to be, then we have to do three things. First, we get you into protective custody. Second, we find out who's doing this. It could be her or someone working for her or a family member." "She didn't have any family." Ryan interrupted. "Neither did we." Troy replied. Ryan nodded in agreement.

And third, we have to prove they're connected without implicating you. "So, where do we start?" Ryan asked. "With Sean. There aren't a lot of drugs that can cause a heart attack. If he was drugged, we'll know for sure." Troy stood and hugged Ryan. "You're going to get through this. Alive! Now, where's all the research you've done trying to find her? We got a lot of work to do." "One more thing." Ryan said as he sat down. "I told you I didn't touch her. That wasn't the truth." Ryan lowered his head. He couldn't look at Troy. "They made me. They said if I didn't, they couldn't trust me not to tell and if they couldn't trust me, they'd kill me." Troy backed away from Ryan and said, "I knew you lied. Not at first, but I've learned a lot since being on the job. I knew there was no way they'd let you walk away as just a witness and not an accomplice. I figured that's why you go so hard for the kids. I'm happy you finally had the balls to tell me the truth. Now let's see if we can find out who killed them and save you."

Misty sat at her sketching desk, staring at the blank pages. She hadn't heard anything about Sean's death. She knew heart attack victims didn't usually make it to the front page, but she needed to know what happened. Killing him that way wasn't good enough and not knowing if he was dead or not was infuriating. She didn't want to Google him. If she ever got caught, that could be used against her. Maybe she could act like she was a client. She could act as a rep for the club and inquire about his company's services. That would be her last resort. She continued to Google the company and see if any news popped up. She decided to go to work early. Sitting there staring at nothing was driving her crazy. After her shift at the club, she met Troy for dinner. She mentioned the most recent story about Kevin and Germaine. There were now seven women that had come forward. He was usually forthcoming with information, but not tonight. He seemed tense and kept trying to change the subject. She didn't know what had changed, but she guessed it had something to do with Sean. Was he dead? Had they made a connection between him, Paul, and Kevin? She tried not to push and be too obvious. He could tell she was curious about his change in demeanor. "We'll talk later." he said. They finished their dinner quietly. Troy tried to start several conversations, but his reluctance to discuss Kevin's case had made things weird. Misty wondered nervously what caused it. She knew it wasn't her or they wouldn't be sitting here trying not to be awkward. It must be Ryan. Had he confessed to Troy after Sean died? That had to be it. But if he confessed, what did Troy say or do? Did he arrest him, punch him, kick him in the balls? Misty shook her head, trying to shake the thoughts away. What if he hadn't done anything but listen? Did she want to be with a man like that? She looked up when she realized Troy was talking to her. "I'm sorry. What did you say?" She asked. "Are you ready to go?" he asked, clearly annoyed that she wasn't listening to him. They left the restaurant and got an Uber to his place. As soon as they got in, he poured himself a drink and another and another. "Whoa!" She said, "Take it easy! What's going on? You've been weird all night. Are you breaking up with me or something?" "What!? No!" Troy said as he slid down off the arm of the couch onto the cushions. "I have something to tell you. Is it gonna sound crazy, but just listen. It was dumped on my lap, and I don't know what to do. You're the only one I can trust." "What about Ryan?" Misty asked. "He's the one that dumped it on me. Come sit down and bring the bottle." He pointed at the vodka bottle. Troy told Misty how he and Ryan met. He'd told her this story before, but this time he included the story Ryan had told him about the attack and the fight they had after. Misty's heart swelled at hearing this part. She knew he was a good man. Then Troy got to the most recent talk with Ryan about the murders of Kevin and Paul and how Sean's death seemed natural but put together with the others probably wasn't. He told her Ryan's theory that it was the girl they'd attacked or her family. When he was finished, she sat silent. Ryan had put it together. She thought he might, but hearing it said out loud was a lot. Knowing that he said it out loud to someone else was even crazier still.

Troy told her how Ryan had agonized over what they'd done for years. How he didn't date much or sleep because of it and how that night had led him to work with troubled youth. He was trying to keep them from making the mistakes he did. He also said Ryan was still searching for her to this day. Misty began to cry. He probably thought she was crying because she felt bad for Ryan and the girl they'd attacked, or maybe even the other guys. But she was crying because she was happy. Happy that Ryan was miserable. Happy that he'd been searching for her all these years. Happy that he was afraid. She had spent all these years feeling isolated and alone. She'd endured so much pain and misery. To find out that at least one of them felt a little of what she felt every day overwhelmed her with emotion. She sobbed so loudly that she had to get up and go into the bathroom to hide the fact that behind her tears, she was beginning to laugh. "He's afraid? Of little old me?" She said to the mirror. She hadn't known exactly how much hatred she'd been holding onto until now. She realized she'd been holding Ryan to a different level of accountability because she had a crush on him, and they were friends. She let herself believe that the other guys were more at fault, but the truth was the opposite, he was her friend and theirs. He knew what type of boys they were. Maybe he didn't think it would go that bad, but he knew it wasn't going to be an innocent game of hide and seek. So what, if he felt guilty after and distanced himself from them. What's done is done and nothing can take it back. The tears and laughs stopped. She was furious now. Troy beat him up, but he was still his friend. He didn't turn him into the cops, or any of them for that matter. He's okay with his friend being a rapist because he's sorry. She thought about killing him right then and there in his apartment, but she'd definitely get caught and if she really wanted him to suffer, killing his best friend was the perfect way to make that happen. Especially now that he knew it was coming and he wouldn't be able to stop it. Misty got her emotions under control before she went back into the living room, or so she thought. "Are you okay babe?" Troy asked as he stood and hugged her. "It's just crazy!" She said, "Ryan seems like such a good guy." "He is!" Troy retorted. "He just got caught up with the wrong crew." "So, he's a follower? Is he only a good guy now because he's following you?" Misty said sharply. "Whoa, whoa! He's trying to make it right, but he can't find her." "How exactly would he do that? Can he un-rape her? Can he un-beat her? And you? You're a police officer! How are you okay with this? Why didn't you turn him in? What if she's dead? That's murder!" She was screaming at this point. Troy just stood there looking at her. He had thought she would be upset but not with him. He wasn't there when it happened. He'd tried to help Ryan find her, but he'd never thought of turning him in. "What if they had killed her? People die of injuries days later all the time." "But she was in the hospital!" he said. "Didn't he say she left early? It doesn't matter. The point is that you are okay with it!" She yelled. She gathered her things. She hadn't planned to argue with him like this. She didn't know if a slip of the tongue would give her away, but she had chosen her words wisely despite being more hurt and upset than she'd ever been since that night. "Misty!" Troy said her name, but nothing else would come out. She was right. But he felt like he and Ryan weren't completely wrong, either. Yes, Ryan had been a part of a terrible thing, but if she wasn't dead... His thoughts trailed off. He looked up when he heard the door close. Misty was gone. He sat there staring at the door. What had just happened? He knew he should go after her, but his body wouldn't move. She was right, he should have called the police when Ryan told him the first time, but nothing would have happened except maybe Ryan would have been expelled. Maybe he would have been expelled himself and sued for slander. Ryan's family was wealthy and connected. That wasn't the point, though. He didn't even think of turning Ryan in. He saw how hurt and afraid he was. He was not a bad guy then or now. He just got caught up in a terrible situation. Troy sat in the same spot all night. He had lost the love of his life and the only way to get her back was to turn against his best friend. "My brother." He said to the empty room, "he's, my brother." Troy was confused when he woke up on the couch with an empty bottle next to him. "Why?" He started to say to Misty but stopped when he realized he was alone. His head was throbbing. He got up to get some water and the scene from the night before played in his head. "What am I gonna do?" He asked himself.

Misty wasn't feeling so good when she woke up, either. She didn't have a hangover but what she felt was worse. Her heart was broken. She walked out on Troy, and he didn't try to stop her. When she left his building, she stood across the street waiting to see if he'd come running out screaming her name. He didn't. She walked to the subway. Now she didn't know if she was hurt because of losing him or because of the story he told her. Was Ryan a good guy that made the terrible mistake of following his friends? Did he deserve to die? Was that fear he was feeling right now enough torture? "I don't fucking know!" She said as she got out of bed. She had been so sure. So sure, that this was the right course of action, but now she wasn't. "Troy is a decent man. A caring man. He's fair but tough. If he thinks Ryan is a good guy, then maybe he is." She said to her reflection. "But, if life hadn't taught her anything else, it had taught her to trust her instincts. She knew she shouldn't have gone with him into the woods that night, but she liked him and wanted him to like her. "Look how that turned out." She said sarcastically. She was going to have to speak to Ryan herself. Then and only then would she know. Goldie was standing in the hall when she emerged from the bathroom. "You okay Mama?" Goldie said brushing the hair from Misty's face. "No." Misty whimpered. "Troy?" Goldie asked. Misty nodded and began to cry. Goldie wrapped her arms around Misty and guided her to the couch. They sat in silence until the tears stopped. "Did he hurt you?" Goldie asked. "No." Misty replied. "Do you think you can work it out?" Misty shrugged. "Do you want to work it out?" This question made Misty sit up. "I really don't know. I've never been through anything like this before. When things are said, hurtful things. How do you go back to before? How do you not feel that pain every time you see them?" Her eyes pleaded with Goldie's for an answer. Goldie shook her head as tears formed in her own eyes. "I don't know, baby. I wish I had a sassy saying to get you through this, but I don't. This, like many things in life, you have to experience for yourself and maybe more than once. Maybe the right words and actions will make it worth trying. Maybe you move on. The only way you know is to talk to him." Misty hugged her tight and thanked God for her love and her support and just being her mother. Goldie's words were about Troy and yes, she would talk to him eventually, but she was thinking about Ryan in that moment. She needed to talk to him.

Troy knew what he had to do. He didn't want to do it, but he knew he had to. He called

Ryan and told him he was coming over. "Bring a pack." Ryan said, meaning his six-pack of Coronas. He'd already upset Misty by telling her Ryan's story, now he was going to tell Ryan that he broke in his trust and told the only other person he loved in the world. What if he lost them both? When Troy got to Ryan's apartment, he stood in front of the door for a few minutes before he knocked. He still wasn't sure how he was going to tell him. He wasn't sure of anything right now. He knocked on the door. When Ryan opened it and he saw the concern on his face. Troy blurted it out before he knew what he was saying. "I told Misty, I told her everything. I needed to talk to someone, and she's the only person I can trust, and I know, I know it puts you at risk, but if you're right about this, you're already at risk and I just didn't know what to do. I always know what to do, but not this time." He was so out of breath when he stopped talking that he had to sit down. Ryan was quiet. He didn't understand what was going on. His best friend had betrayed him by telling his girlfriend of less than a year his most private, personal, and dangerous secret. Not to mention he was possibly being hunted by a serial killer. He felt dizzy and plopped down on the couch next to Troy. He wanted to punch him, but he didn't have enough energy. "What did she say?" Ryan asked. Troy let out a long sigh and told Ryan how it had gone. "Have you spoken to her?" Ryan asked. "No." Troy answered. "I don't know what to say to her. "Tell her you made it all up! That you're a pathological liar or crazy or delusional or something!" Ryan made a sound. At first Troy thought he was crying, but when he looked over at him and he saw that he was laughing. Troy stared at him as the laughter got stronger and louder. Soon he joined in, and they both laughed so hard they had tears in their eyes. "What are we gonna do?" Ryan managed to get out. "Man, I don't fucking know." Troy replied. "This is more fucked up than anything I could imagine. How about we just skip town for a few years?" Ryan laughed some more. "Where would we go? What would we do?" Troy threw his hands up and shook his head. "We can get in the car and drive like those chicks in that movie." Ryan's laughing has subsided. He said, "Bro, we don't have a car." They burst into laughter again. When the laughter died down, they sat in silence. Ryan broke it and said, "Bro, I get it. I don't like it, but I get why you told her. Now you have to fix it. For your sake and mine. I can't be worried about all this at once and you love her. She loves you, too. Call her." He punched him in the arm. "That's for being a blabbermouth. Where is the beer?" Ryan said, looking around. Troy said, "I figured if we got through this talk, we'd need something stronger."

The next day, Misty took a walk. It was one of her favorite type of days, misty and warm for March. She walked and thought about this path she was on and how things that were so clear before weren't anymore. She hadn't heard from Troy since their blow up the other night. She hadn't reached out to him, but she thought he would have tried to call her or at least send a text saying I'm sorry or something by now. "Did I break up with Reggie too early?" She thought, I can use some comforting words right now. She laughed at the thought of that conversation. "I need a hug cause my killing spree isn't going as planned." She continued to walk as her thoughts turned to Ryan and exactly how she was going to approach him. Maybe he'd come to her if Troy told him he spilled the beans. He'd have to tell him. He didn't know if she was going to report them. Of course, she wouldn't do that because that would bring too much attention to her and the murders. Right now, they were random deaths as far as the police were concerned, and she needed it to stay that way. Before she knew it, she was back at her building. Her feet were on autopilot. She'd start following Ryan tomorrow and play the approaching him part by ear. As for Troy, maybe distance was better because if she killed Ryan, she didn't want to see the fallout.

Ryan sat at his kitchen table the next morning, replaying his conversation with Troy. His life was spiraling out of control. On one hand, he felt like it was overdue. You can't do what they'd done and not expect it to come back on you. On the other hand, he had worked so hard for years trying to pay it back. Okay, he hadn't found her to make it up to her specifically, but he'd done the best he could. What was the bill for something like that, though? Could it ever be paid? What if she had died from her injuries? So many questions and no answers. Troy was still sleeping it off on the couch. "Thank God you didn't throw up Bro!" He said to his sleeping friend. He really loved

Misty if he had gone to her for counsel about this. "So, you should stop crushing on her." He said to himself. He still wasn't sure if it was a crush. She seemed so familiar to him, and he couldn't figure out why or shake it off. He had way too many things going on right now to be thinking about her, but she was always present in his thoughts. Those eyes! Tupac wrote a poem called "Because I've seen your soul before". That's how he felt about Misty. He wanted to talk to her alone. He couldn't tell Troy how he felt, and his questions would probably get personal if he ever had the chance to talk to her, so Troy could not be there. He wanted, no, needed to know who she really was and where she was from. He knew she grew up in foster care, but not where. She came to the city around 10 years ago, but there was no record of her before then. Yes, he ran a background check on her and no, he hadn't told Troy. Runaways changed their names all the time, though. He could try to get her fingerprints, but they would only produce a hit if she'd been arrested or worked with kids or something like that. Most people were never fingerprinted. He was determined to find a way to get what he needed. It may take a little time. He giggled to himself, "You may not have time, Bro." Troy moved on the couch. "Oh, so you are alive. I was starting to worry." Ryan said to Troy as he sat up. "Shut up." Troy replied, holding his head. "How much did we drink?" "Oh no, not we Bro. You! How much did you drink? You were looking for all the answers to life's questions at the bottom of that bottle last night. Did you find them?" Ryan said jokingly. Troy stood up and headed to the bathroom. He flipped Ryan the bird as he passed. "Don't blame me cause you don't know your limit." Ryan said laughing. "Get it together. We have a game at three."

12

Misty was at the club when Troy called.
"Hello?" she answered. "Hey, um. I wasn't sure
you would answer. You have that show tonight,
right? Well, I just wanted to see if we could meet
up and talk about things." Troy said. "You sure
you wanna do that? It didn't go so well last time.
Sorry." Misty answered. "What are you sorry for?"
He asked. "I know it took a lot for you to tell me
all that, and I had a complete meltdown." "Yeah,
I'm coming." Misty said to someone in the room."
"That's why we need to talk. I could have handled
it better, too. How's tomorrow sound?" He asked.
"I'll call you back and I'll let you know." Misty said
as she ended the call. She was very busy and still
very upset with him for not coming after her. She
wanted to say, "Yes, I'll see you tomorrow." But
she couldn't give in that easily. She was fitting the
Queens for the show. Ralph and Renee were
supposed to be helping but all they'd done so far

was cause distractions. She loved them, but she really needed them to focus. "Hey guys! Look, I really need your help." she said. "Okay Mama. Why you so stressed? We got lots of time." Renee said. "No, we don't! I have to make sure the wardrobe is done, and you promised that you'd help with the set, but you guys are just dancing and playing around!" She yelled a little more harshly than she intended. Renee's smile faded. "I'm sorry, Mama. We always play around, but you know we get to it, eventually." he said. "Yes, but I need you to get it done now. I have too much on my plate today and I just need you to do what I ask." Misty said. Ralph came back into the room. They saw how stressed she was and hugged her. "Okay, no more playtime." Renee said, "Let's get this done." Ralph asked Renee what happened?" I don't know. Something's got her tits twisted, so let's just get the work done and get out of here." Renee answered. A few hours later, when everything was done, she apologized and so did they. They hugged it out like they always did after an argument.

Troy and Ryan took the team out after the game. They always took them out, win or lose.

They wanted them to see that hard work paid off, but they'd won the game tonight, so they were celebrating. Troy tried to join in the celebration, but his talk with Misty was all he could think about. He had hoped he'd picked the right time to call her, but he hadn't. He knew she was busy, and he was nervous. He should have waited until he had rehearsed what he was going to say or at least until the next day. He was rambling like an idiot. He never rambled. This girl was turning him into a different person. "This girl?" He said to himself. "This love, you mean. You're in love and this is what love does to you." He sat back in his seat. Ryan looked at him and laughed. "In the words of the famous poet Usher, you got it bad!" He said, slapping Troy on the arm. "Here, eat your pizza." He pushed the plate in front of Troy.

After the show, Misty was wiped out. She had been so busy she had forgotten to eat and was feeling a little lightheaded. She grabbed a bag of chips on her way home. Now she was tearing through last night's leftovers. As she ate, she thought about Troy. She always thought about Troy. She wanted to call him, but she didn't know what to say. Apparently, he didn't either. She'd never heard him sound like that. "Is this what love does to you?" She thought. She'd have to speak to him, eventually. "Do I?" she asked herself. If she broke up with him, she wouldn't have to deal with the aftermath of Ryan's death. The conversation with Troy had given her more reasons to doubt if she could kill Ryan. Was he remorseful for what he'd done? Had he really been looking for her? There were a lot of holes in his story, though. Maybe he forgot or blocked it out. Trauma does that. "Trauma. Do attackers feel trauma? Do murderers feel trauma?" she asked the empty room. She wished she could talk to him. Just him, so she could feel him out. She didn't see how that would play out, though. So many things could go wrong. "Fuck it." She said to herself. Things went wrong all the time, and she managed to work through it. This was too important of a decision to make without having all the information. She had to know for certain. She sent Troy a text asking for Ryan's number. She said she needed to ask him a legal question. When he saw the text was from her, he got excited until he read it. She wanted to talk to Ryan about a legal question. "Yeah right." He thought. He texted her Ryan's number. "I told

148

him I told you." He texted. She didn't reply. It took her three days to contact Ryan, and she still didn't know what she was going to say. She really liked Ryan when they were kids. They would go for walks and talk about what they'd do and what they'd be when they grew up. He said he wished his parents could adopt her, so she didn't have to live at the group home anymore. He was her best friend and then things changed. When he became a senior, he started hanging out with some new boys. At first, they seemed like they were okay, but then she noticed that he wouldn't speak to her if they were around. He'd just wave like she was just some girl. One of them would make fun of her when Ryan wasn't around. A few times, they had plans to meet, and he didn't show up. So, when he asked her to hang out with them that night, she was excited. She missed being around him. She shook the memory out of her head. She was going to talk to him and decide after looking him in his eyes while he told her the story of what they'd done to her. That was the only way she'd know for sure. She sent him a text asking him to meet her at the club. He said he was busy with work, but he could meet her at his place the next day around 8:00 o'clock. She agreed. She wasn't sure how hearing him tell the story would make her feel. She never considered that she'd have to talk to any of them about that night. Not like a conversation where she'd hear their point of view. Whose idea, was it? Did they talk about it before? How long did they talk about it after? Were they proud of themselves? Were they scared? She had never thought about how they'd been affected by their actions. They were the bad guys. Their feelings didn't matter. Did they? She was the victim, and nobody cared about her feelings. Bad guys didn't get to cry about their crimes. "I was a kid!" She yelled into the empty room. "So was he." she whispered. If he wasn't in on it, if he didn't know that's what they were planning, was he also a victim? Misty sat down and cried. She had never considered that could have been the case. Her pain and embarrassment had never allowed her to see it from any other perspective. She couldn't afford to see it any other way. She was fueled by her pain. It had gotten her this far, but maybe it was time to try something else. Misty woke up in the middle of the night in a cold sweat. She had dreamed about that night again, but this time there was an extra scene. This time she saw Ryan's eyes and the pain in them. Was she making that up now that she knew that he'd been looking for her? She reminded herself to remain objective until she met with him and listened to his story. She realized that she didn't want to kill Ryan. She wanted to believe that he had truly been her friend back then and that he was a victim, too. He hadn't stopped them but maybe he tried. Maybe they forced him to take his turn. She would find out tomorrow and then she'd decide. He probably wouldn't have been able to stop them even if he did try. It would've been three to one, and Ryan was the one.

Ryan told Troy that Misty was coming over. They both agreed that Troy should not show up and that she probably wanted to talk about what he'd done and maybe get some relationship advice. They met at their favorite spot around 4:00 and went over every question they thought Misty might ask. Ryan said, "Bro I'm just gonna be honest with her. I fucked up! I'm sorry that this is coming back on you, but you brought her in to this when you told her. I understand why you told her. You were my outlet, and she was yours. Now we're all swimming in this shit together." Troy had mixed emotions about them meeting. On the one hand he figured this meant she still wanted to be with him. She could've shut him out completely, but she wanted to talk. On the other hand, she may be judging him by Ryan's actions, so if she didn't like what Ryan had to say it would be over. They parted ways and Troy went back to work. There was no way he could sit at home waiting for Ryan to call.

To get ready for her evening, Misty went for a walk. She didn't go to Central Park because the trains were backed up again. Instead, she walked to the Westside highway and strolled uptown. She stopped and watched the boats go by. "What if I hid on one of those and just started over wherever it was going? You'd probably die before you got there. Die of starvation or thirst or cold. Wait, I think that last one is what happens when you hide on a plane." Misty looked up and saw that she was near a couple, and they probably heard her talking to herself. She smiled at them and tapped her ear. "Thank God for your buds!" She thought and giggled. She had often thought of leaving New York, but she couldn't just leave

Goldie and the twins without explaining. They would assume the worst and be sick with worry. She was blessed to have them. She wondered if they would move with her. She could see them all living in LA. No, they'd never agree to that. Their lives were here and so was hers. She didn't want to leave and if tonight went well, she wouldn't have to. If she didn't have to kill Ryan, she could stay in New York with Troy and live happily ever after. She giggled. The fact that she could still believe in happily ever after was hilarious and sad. "It's the God in me!" she sang to herself. Yes, some terrible things had happened to her, but there had also been some amazing and beautiful things. She sighed. "That's what life is." She said to herself. "Lemons or lemonade. We'll see which one tonight turns out to be."

Troy was at the precinct. That was the only place he could go that might keep his mind off Misty and Ryan's meeting. "Maybe I can hide in the closet." He'd said to Ryan earlier. "Hell no!" Ryan said, laughing. "She'd never trust you again. Look, I'm your best friend. I've got your back. She'll back in your arms real soon. Trust me!" Troy knew he was right, but there was so much riding on things going well tonight. "Please God, don't let me lose her." He prayed. Troy sat at his desk wishing for something to take his mind off their meeting when the call came in. He quickly regretted his wish for a distraction. Some kids had robbed a Bodega. They weren't armed, but the owner was. He shot one kid in the back as he ran away. The owner had been arrested and the kids, all but one, had run off. He was also in custody. There were cameras in the store and out front. He hated watching videos of someone's last moments. That was something no one should ever get used to, and this was a kid. "Be careful what you wish for." He scolded himself as he grabbed his things off his desk. The notifications were the worst. Telling someone that their loved one was dead was not something they could teach you. Experience was the only way to learn. He always did the notifications on his cases. He didn't like the uniformed officers to do it. Not because of them personally. It was the uniform. Some people became defensive at the sight of the uniform and that, in turn made the officers defensive and things just went downhill from there. So tonight, he'd notify a family that their worst nightmares

had come true and then go drink himself to sleep.
"Be careful what you wish for." He said again.

13

Misty arrived at Ryan's apartment and stood in front of his door for a few seconds before she knocked. He had buzzed her up so she couldn't back out, but she needed to steady herself. She was about to enter the apartment of the last of her attackers. She had dreamed and planned about this for so long and now she was here, but not as a killer. Not as one of her aliases, but as herself. Not the girl he knew, but who she was today. "Worst murder spree ever!" she whispered to herself as she knocked on the door. Ryan had the table set and wine glasses on the countertop next to a bottle on ice. It looked like he had prepared for a date, not a meeting. Well, maybe this was how people prepared for a casual meeting. That's what this was, after all. A meeting to discuss what Troy had told her and probably a little about them getting back together. That's what the twins told her. "Girl, he's gonna try to convince you to stay with his boy! Unless he has the hots for you! Then that could get messy. Oh, can we go? We love messy!" Rene said. She laughed as Ralph slapped him on the back of his head. She had told them about the dinner and the tension between herself and Troy, but not about Ryan's story. They were waiting on standby if she called, but she didn't think she needed any help tonight. If things went wrong, she couldn't risk them seeing what she was going to do. After Misty left Renee said. "We should follow her. What if he tries something?" Ralph shook his head and replied in a whisper. "If he does, it'll be the last thing he ever does. But we ain't gonna follow her. She can handle herself." Ralph had noticed the change in her. A confidence that wasn't there before. One day they were talking, and he asked if she ever thought about the guys that attacked her and she said, "Not anymore". There was something about how she said it that gave him a chill. He knew she had taken self-defense classes and that sometimes she disappeared for hours, but he hadn't put too much thought into it until then. Could she? Would she? He tried to remember the names of the guys that attacked her, but he couldn't remember. Had she ever told them their names to start with? He couldn't remember that either. "Boy, please!" He laughed at himself. "Misty a murderer, no! My imagination is wild! I should write a book." "Okay, well if we're not gonna follow her let's go eat." Renee said.

Misty sat at the table across from Ryan, trying to control her heart rate. "Thanks for meeting with me." Misty said. "I've been wanting to talk to you since Troy told me, well, you know. I'm sure he told you how I reacted." Misty said. "Yeah, he did. I don't blame you, really." Ryan said, "We need to discuss that and this thing with you and Troy." Ryan said, pouring them both a glass of wine. Misty nodded. The twins were right. Of course, he wanted to talk about her and Troy. Ryan took a drink and said, "I have a confession to make. I think about you a lot. At first, I thought I had a crush on you, but then I realized it wasn't that. It's your eyes. They seem so familiar to me. I know we hadn't met before Troy introduced us, but it's been bugging me since that night." Misty just stared at him. She was stunned because she had wondered if he recognized her, and he did. Sort of. Where did you grow up? He asked.

"Philadelphia. She replied. "Then that can't be it." he said. "I don't think I would have forgotten you." She replied "Yeah, I'm pretty unforgettable." Ryan said and laughed. Misty joined in the laughter. She was relieved that he'd made a joke and not gone the more serious route. "Sorry I make corny jokes when I'm nervous." he said, still laughing. "Maybe you just remind me of someone." Yeah, that must be it. I just wanted to put that out there in case you caught me staring at you." Misty didn't say anything because she didn't know what to say. She had to choose her words carefully. She didn't know what would pop out of her mouth. They sat in an awkward silence for a while. Misty broke the silence and said, "So, tell me what happened that night. Troy already told you." Ryan replied. "He did, but that's what he remembered from what you told him. I want to hear it from you." she said. "Why?" he asked. "So I can see and hear what Troy did. He believes that you were tricked into it and that you sincerely regret it. If you want me to believe that I need to hear it from you." Tears were welling up in her eyes and Ryan just stared at her. Why was she crying? Was it for him or for the girl in the story?

Why did her eyes look so familiar? These questions were running through his mind as he began speaking. He was describing their friendship and how much he liked her. "What was her name?" Misty interrupted. "Michelle." He answered. Now his eyes were filled with tears. He talked for what felt like hours. Smiling and laughing at some of his memories. Misty had to control the urge and jump in and correct him when he got some of the details wrong. She enjoyed hearing him recount their past with such fondness. Then he got to that night and the details she didn't know about. They really had tricked him into inviting her. He sobbed while telling this part of their story and so did she. He told her how he distanced himself from them after that night and where the prostitute story came from. He told her how he'd been searching for her ever since. She wanted to say "Here I am! I'm right here! But she couldn't. How would he react? Stunned, of course. Happy maybe. They'd have questions on top of questions on top of questions. But eventually he or Troy or both of them would put it together that she'd killed the others and come after her. "What would you say to her if you found her?" Misty asked, breaking the silence again. Her question seemed to take him by surprise. "I, I, I don't know." Ryan stuttered. "Yes, you do." Misty said. "You don't search for someone as long as you have and not have an idea of what you'd say. I bet you played it out in your head many times." He just stared at her. She was right, of course. "You say that like you're speaking from experience." he said. "A little." she said, "We all have people from our past that if given the chance we'd have choice words for. Not always bad, though. You know, like someone that was nice to you, but you never got the chance to thank them." Ryan nodded and said, "Yeah, I guess you're right. I guess I'd tell her sorry. Sorry for leading you up there, sorry for letting them do that to you." Misty listened to him, waiting for him to say what he'd done to her. She grew angry when she realized he wasn't going to tell that part. She regretted meeting with him, but there was no backing out now. "Is that it?" she asked. "How about sorry for kicking you! Sorry for raping you!" Misty had stood up and was pacing back and forth. "Your story has some holes in it, Ryan. You want me to pity you? Poor Ryan got tricked into being a rapist. What about her? That poor child. She was scared, and she looked to you for help." Ryan looked at her, puzzled. "What do you mean holes? That's the way it happened Troy must have gotten some stuff wrong." he said. Misty paused and gave him a look that made him shiver. She said, "No, he told me your bullshit version, word for word. That's one of the reasons I know it's a lie." Ryan said, "I told him everything that happened. Wat, what do you mean one reason? Why do you think it's a lie." Misty held up her hand and stopped him from talking. "You said you didn't touch her. That's not true, is it, Ryan? Now maybe they made you take your turn, but you raped her. You kicked her." "How? Was all Ryan could manage to say. "How do you think?" Misty said. "No, you can't be. You can't be her!" he said. "Why can't I be? Because you killed her? Because she didn't look like this?" She said, pointing to her face. "I was afraid to meet you. I thought you'd recognize me and that it would be over, but you didn't. I know I look different, but I thought" she trailed off. "I sat in that hospital alone. Blaming myself for being fooled by you. I thought you were my friend!" She yelled. "The others?" Ryan asked, "Yeah that was me." Misty answered. "You were next, but then I met Troy and he just happened to be your friend. Your best friend! What are the odds? When he told me your story, I had to talk to you, I thought maybe he doesn't have to die. Maybe he really is sorry." "I am!" Ryan said. He tried to get up, but he wasn't able to stand. "What's wrong with me?" He asked. "I gave you a little something. I came here with an open mind, but better safe than sorry."

Although Misty had prayed that the night would go well, she planned for the opposite. When Ryan had got up to go to the bathroom, she put a few drops of a slow acting sedative in his drink. Still hoping for the best, she figured she'd let herself out, and he'd think he just drank too much. When Troy told her the story, she noted that Ryan had left out his part in her attack, or maybe Troy just didn't tell her that part. She thought she would be okay with it because it was one thing to be tricked into doing something horrible and something totally different to be a willing participant. Had he left out those parts or blocked them out? But now, as she stood there looking at him, she knew that didn't matter. He asked her to go up there. He raped her. He beat her. He lied and went on with his life. "You beat me so bad that I didn't even recognize myself when the bandages came off." She said as tears fell from her eyes. "Nope, not crying. I didn't want this to go this way. I wanted you to be a victim just like me, but you're not. You hesitated at first, but you joined in. You caved to the pressure!" "No, I didn't! Ryan interrupted. "They said they'd kill me." "Yes, you did! Misty said through her teeth. "Maybe they made you, but you got into it. I remember every kick and punch. The painful rapes over and over. I cried for you to help me. My friend, my love!" Ryan sat silently crying on the couch. Could what she was saying be true? "I'm sorry." He whispered, "I'm so, so sorry. I knew your eyes were familiar, but I never thought." He trailed off. "How is this you?" Ryan asked. "The wonders of plastic surgery." Misty answered. "I was afraid." Ryan said. "They said if I didn't join in, they killed me!" "So, it was me or you and you chose you." Misty said. "I get it. You could've told the truth to the police, but you didn't. This poor me routine. I can't. You could have written an anonymous letter to the police.

You could have claimed to be an eyewitness that didn't want to come forward. There's always someone who sees something, but you did nothing. You went on about your life like it never happened." This time, she let the tears fall. Ryan's phone rang. It was Troy, he had been calling both their phones for the past hour. "All right, I gotta think. I gotta get out of here." Misty said. "He knows you're here." Ryan said weekly. "Yeah, but he doesn't know who I am." Ryan tried one last time to get up but fell onto the floor and passed out. Misty took his phone just in case and went into the bedroom. She went through his clothes looking for a disguise and she hit the jackpot. All his clothes were way too big for her but there was a bag of basketball uniforms that were closer to her size. They probably belonged to the kids on the team. This building had cameras in the lobby and in the elevators so she couldn't leave that way, but she remembered Reggie telling her that most buildings don't have cameras on the trash exits because they were usually exit only and nobody cared about people going through trash. So, she would leave out the trash exit and come back in dressed in the clothes she found pretending to be a delivery person. Before she left, she called the concierge desk and told him they were expecting a delivery and to let them bring it upstairs. Ryan had done this earlier for a package that he was expecting. She tied Ryan up with some of his neck ties and left. She'd kill him later. She needed his time of death to be after the delivery person entered the building. She wasn't sure how accurate the coroner would be, but just in case. She grabbed a bag from a previous food delivery, disabled the slam lock and closed the door. She took the stairs to avoid the cameras in the elevator and slipped out the back of the building unseen. She walked a few blocks and dipped into an ally to change clothes. When she returned to Ryan's building, she looked and sounded like a different person. She imitated a character she'd seen on TV with a high-pitched voice that talked nonstop. It worked perfectly. When she got back to the apartment, Ryan was still out cold. He looked so peaceful. Misty cried. She didn't have to clean up her DNA this time. She allowed herself to let go. She allowed herself to imagine what could have been. The friendship or love life they could have shared had they both made different decisions. She grabbed the trophy from the shelf and beat him with it. Then she took a pillow and smothered him. She was careful not to punch him. She didn't want any bruises on her hands to match his bruises. She reversed her steps and exited the building as the fast-talking delivery person and reentered as herself through the trash exit. She had left it slightly open. She took the stairs and went back to Ryan's apartment. She threw some things around and knocked others down to make it look like a fight had occurred. Now it was her turn. She put her head in the refrigerator and closed it on herself several times. She also needed to look like a fight had occurred. She smashed both of their phones and waited for Troy to arrive. If he wasn't there in 30 minutes, she would go downstairs and alert the concierge.

Misty laid on the floor going over her story. She was just about to go to the door when Troy started knocking. She started to moan and cry when she heard him at the door. After a few more knocks, the door opened. Troy was Ryan's emergency contact person, so the concierge was allowed to let him in. "Oh no!" he yelled when he saw Misty on the floor. "What happened?

Where's Ryan?" He asked her. She raised her arm weakly and pointed to the room. "Go check the room!" He yelled at the concierge. The concierge went into the room while he attended to Misty. "Who did this to you?" He asked. Misty pretended to try to talk. Troy was on his phone calling for the police and an ambulance when the concierge came back. He was pale and looked like he was going to be sick. "What is it? Where is he?" Troy yelled. He, he, he's dead." The concierge stuttered. "What?" Troy yelled. "Baby, I'll be right back!" He said, laying Misty against the couch. Troy ran into the room almost knocked the concierge down. He stopped when he saw Ryan's body. His eyes were open, and his legs and arms were tied. He gently touched his neck to check for a pulse. There wasn't one. He dropped to his knees. He reached out to touch him, but then his training kicked in. "Get out!" He said as he stood and backed away from his best friend's body. The police would arrive soon, and he didn't want to contaminate the scene any more than they already had. He went back to Misty. "What happened?" He asked her again. "She." Misty said, and she started shaking her head and crying. She looked pleadingly into Troy's eyes, and he held her to him. "It's Okay. You can tell us later at the hospital." Misty nodded her head and said, "Ryan?" "You just relax. Help will be here soon. We'll talk about everything once you get checked out." He said as he held her. Misty felt his tears dropping on her face.

When the police and the EMTs arrived, Misty saw firsthand how they worked the crime scene. The whole thing was so overwhelming that she hyperventilated and passed out. She woke up in the hospital a few hours later and Troy was still there by her side. "Oh, thank God!" He said, when he saw she was awake. "You scared me! I thought I'd lost you too!" He said as he kissed her hand. "Do you remember what happened?" He asked." I think so. Ryan? Where is Ryan?" She said with panic in her voice. Troy held her hand and gently told her that Ryan was dead. "No, no, no, no!" She said shaking her head. The pain that shot through her head was excruciating. She winced and put her hands on her head. "The doc said you have a concussion. So, you gotta take it slow for a few days." Troy told her. "Oh, is that why I feel like this?" She asked. "Yeah. I'm sorry." he said. "No,

I'm sorry. Ryan is like your brother. I'm sorry, baby." She said as she grabbed his hand. She didn't have to fake moving slow. They must have given her some drugs for the pain. She felt woozy. She'd have to be careful about what she said when they questioned her. "I can't believe this happened. I should have been there!" Troy said through his tears. "Do you remember what happened? Who did this?" He asked. "We ordered takeout and when the food came, a woman was there, and she did something to him when he opened the door." Misty had rehearsed this in her head so much that saying it out loud made it feel like it had really happened. "What do you mean?" Troy asked. "He said something and then he fell backwards. She came in and hit me with something. She was so fast. I must have passed out cause when I woke up, they were in the room, and she was yelling at him." Misty recounted her story. "What was she yelling?" Troy asked. "Something about payback, I think." Misty stopped and cupped her face with her hands, and she cried. "Payback? Payback for what?" Troy was mumbling. Then he stopped. "No, no it can't be." he said. "What is it?" Misty asked. "That story I told you about." He moved closer to her and spoke in a low voice. "The thing that we argued about, the other guys that were involved. They all died recently. They were murdered. Ryan thought they might be connected. I told him it was ridiculous. They didn't even know each other anymore, and the girl was probably dead. Ryan had been searching for her for years. I told you. It can't be." He trailed off. "I didn't know." Misty said. "I thought he was being paranoid because those guys were into some kinky shit and I figured, well, we figured that's what got them killed." he said. "We?" Misty asked. "The other detectives and me. I looked into it. I read the files. They didn't seem connected, and those guys." He trailed off again, shaking his head. "Look, the detectives that are assigned to your case are going to question you. Don't mention that last part about his suspicions. I'll handle that part. I have to talk to my captain about this. A serial killer changes the landscape." Ryan's tone had changed. He was in cop mode now. Misty shuddered at the title serial killer. She hadn't thought of herself like that. She was on a killing spree, but she wasn't a serial killer. Didn't they kill random people for no reason? Was there a difference? Probably not in the eyes of the law or Troy. Wasn't she entitled to revenge? Whatever you called it, a serial killer or spree killer, a killer is what she was now. "I am what they made me." She said to herself.

When the detectives showed up, they asked Troy to leave. He said he would go down to the morgue and check with the coroner. Misty told her story, and they asked questions, a lot of questions, but they didn't seem to suspect her. Troy came back after the detectives left. He offered to stay the night, but Misty told him to go home. He had spoken to Ryan's parents, and he'd called Goldie. She could only imagine how Goldie had reacted. He said he had convinced her not to come tonight by promising to have Misty call her. She hated that she had done this to him. He left reluctantly and promised to be back as soon as he could. He had a very long day ahead of him.

The next morning, Goldie, Ralph and Renee came in. "Oh my God Misty, are you okay!? I mean, is anything broken? Did he?" Goldie was saying. "No, no! I'm just a little banged up, and it wasn't Ryan. It was a woman." Misty interrupted. Ralph said, "A woman? Why would she do that?

He's dead, right?" "You're lucky she didn't kill you too!" Misty said, "I don't think she expected him to have company." "She banged you up pretty bad, though!" Goldie said as she touched Misty's face and started to cry. "Don't cry, I'm okay. They say I'll be here a few days for observation, but I should be fine." Misty said. The twins were fighting over her dessert and stealing rubber gloves, so they clearly weren't too concerned about her. That was good because Misty needed them to help calm Goldie down. They stayed until visiting hours were over. When they were leaving Renee asked, "Where are your clothes? We can take them home and clean them." "The cops took them as evidence Misty replied. "Oh, no, not the limited-edition Nikes! I told you not to wear those!" Renee said. "Yeah, cause you knew she would get attacked, and they'd end up in an evidence locker!" Ralph said, shaking his head. Misty choked on her water when he said this. She had forgotten to change her shoes when she came in the building in disguise. She didn't know how clear the video would be or how wide the shot was, but if it showed those shoes, she was in trouble. Goldie patted her on the back and said,

"Slow down now." Misty felt like she was about to have a full-blown panic attack. They said their goodbyes and promised to return the next day. Misty laid awake most of the night. She couldn't believe that she was in this position again. In the hospital, contemplating running away. The first time was easy. She didn't have family or friends that she'd miss or hurt. This time, though. How could she walk away from them? They'd be heartbroken and confused? She loved her life. She didn't want to walk away from it, but she'd lose it anyway if she got caught. And she couldn't go to jail. "I should never have started this." She said to herself. "You didn't start it. They did. Yeah, but I fucked up. When Troy sees those shoes, he's gonna know it was me." She went over every scenario multiple times. She had money. She'd been stashing away for years. A few years ago, she told herself that she could stop because things were great, and she'd never have to leave. "Good thing I didn't listen to you." She said to herself. She didn't know how much was there, but it would definitely be enough to get out of town and start over somewhere else. She started crying. She didn't want things to go this way. "Worst murder spree ever!" She said, punching the pillow on her lap. She cried as she planned her escape.

Troy's mind was racing. He had gone back to the precinct and called the coroner's office again. They still didn't have any answers for him. Toxicology took time, so he went back to Ryan's building. The cops on scene wouldn't let him in the apartment, so he walked around trying to process everything that had happened. He'd lost his best friend and almost lost the woman he loved. He couldn't believe that Ryan was right about it all being connected. This woman had been waiting in the shadows and researching the guys that attacked her and gotten her revenge. Honestly, he didn't blame her. If someone did that to his sister or mom or Misty, he'd kill them. He had to admit that he accepted Ryan's account of the attack as the truth because he was his friend and when he told him the whole truth, he didn't know what to say. He'd planned on addressing it later, but he was focused on fixing things with Misty first. Well, she clearly hadn't died. But Ryan must have known that to keep searching for her all these years. Something occurred to him. If she had killed those guys, could she have planted all the evidence that led them to the sex clubs? Were they really into all that, or was it just a deterrent? They'd have to start fresh with all their investigations. This was a nightmare. He was going to have to explain everything. Ryan's reputation would be ruined. He hated that part. Ryan had done excellent work in the community and helped so many kids, but now he wouldn't be remembered for any of that. He'd just be another rapist that got what was coming to him. Troy called his captain and briefed him on the night's events and the connection to the other murders. They set up a meeting with the other detectives. It went just how he thought it would. Disbelieving looks at first, then arguments about who would take lead and finally the 'your ass is grass' look from his captain. He knew he could weather just about any storm thrown at him, but this was different. When he talked about his friendship with Ryan and how he first told him about the attack, their faces softened a bit. Every one of them could put themselves in his place. When he spoke about Misty, he almost shed a tear, but there were no wisecracks or jokes. He'd lost his best friend, and the killer had beaten his girl.

These things changed everything. Their connection to him made them family. This was personal.

14

Goldie went back to the hospital the next morning alone. She could tell the twins had been too much for Misty. Misty smiled when she saw her and tried to sit up in bed. "No, no. You stay comfortable. I can talk to you if you're laying down." Goldie said. "How are you?" She asked. "The doc says I may be able to leave tomorrow." Misty said leave instead of go home because she wasn't sure where she was going. "I don't mean that. I mean, how are you? I know this must be bringing up old memories." Goldie said, pointing into the room. "More than you know." Misty thought to herself. "Yeah, it's familiar." She said to Goldie. Goldie placed her hand on Misty's and nodded. They sat in silence for most of the visit. Silence between them had never been awkward. It was like they had a silent language that only they knew, it was filled with understanding and love. When Goldie got up to leave, she kissed

Misty on the forehead and said, "I think I've had enough of New York. How about you?" Misty looked at her with wide eyes. Goldie winked and walked out of the room. Misty's mind was racing. Did she know? How could she? That's not what she meant. Maybe she was sick of the violence in this city. "She knows." Misty said to the room "she knows."

When Goldie left the hospital, she took a cab home and walked around the block a few times before going upstairs. She didn't really want to leave New York, but she couldn't let Misty go and be on her own again. Besides, a change might be good for her. But the twins were a different story. They couldn't go with them, and they definitely couldn't tell them where or why they were going. They would tell the whole thing within minutes. She didn't want to leave them, but they had each other and the girls at the club loved them. They'd be fine. The doc said they would probably let Misty out in a day or two, so she didn't have a lot of time to get things done. She had started preparing for this a few months ago when she discovered what Misty was up to.

She'd hoped it wouldn't come to this, but here they were.

Misty was watching TV when Troy walked in. "Hey Babe!" He said as he kissed her on the forehead. "Hey!" She replied. "What you got for me?" she asked, pointing to the bag he was carrying. "Oh, you mean this?" He said, holding up the bag. "Just the best chicken parm in the city!" "Oh yes!" Misty exclaimed. She was beyond sick of this hospital food already. It was worse than she remembered, even worse than the swill they served at the group home, and she didn't think it could get any worse than that. She sat up and he laid everything out for them. "How did it go with the detectives?" He asked. "Okay, I guess!" Misty shrugged and said, "We went over it like 50 times." "Yeah, that's normal." He said, "You didn't mention that thing, right?" He asked. "No, no. I just told them what happened in the apartment." "Good. I talked to my captain and the other detectives. They weren't happy about starting from scratch, but at least we know we're looking for the same woman." he said. Misty looked confused. "We? They're going to let you investigate. I thought that was against the rules."

she said. "Yeah, it is. I can't officially be a part of the case because of my relationship with Ryan and you, but I have valuable information, so I'm allowed to have access to everything." Troy answered. "Oh, okay." Misty responded. "What do you know about the rules, anyway?" he asked playfully. "I watch Law and Order. I know stuff." Misty said. They both laughed. It was nice to see a real smile on his face. He would survive this. It would be painful, but he would survive.

Goldie made some calls and set things in motion. First was Rachel, her partner at the club. She told her that she was going to take Misty away for a while to clear her head and that she had left a letter outlining everything she needed to know. She also told her that the twins would be staying, and she should use them in any way she needed. The next call was to the twins she asked them to come over because she needed to speak to them urgently. She absolutely could not tell them they were leaving over the phone. They would just show up at the door, anyway. When they arrived, she told them the same thing she told Rachel. "Oh, we're taking a road trip?" Ralph said. "No baby. This trip is just for me and Misty."

Goldie said. "Why can't we go?" He asked. "Look, you know we love you, but you also know that you two can be too much at times. Misty has been through a lot, and she just needs quiet and calm to regroup." Renee was quiet for once. "We can be better. We can be quiet." Ralph said. Goldie gave him a look that said everything. "She's right." Renee finally spoke. "You go and get our girl together and we'll be here when you get back." Goldie kissed them both and said, "Thank you. I love you. I have jobs for you too. I spoke to Rachel, and she'll be expecting you at the club tomorrow to go over all the things you'll need you to do while we're away. Now you'll be taking my place around there, so don't make me look bad." The twins looked at each other and jumped up and screamed, "Hell yeah! Oh, Mama, you know we got this!" Ralph said, smiling. "Okay, here's a list of things that need to be done. Rachel has the same list, so you're all on the same page." Renee asked. "When are you leaving?" "As soon as possible. We won't have our phones, but we'll get in touch with you when we can." Goldie said. "Why not?" Ralph asked. "No distractions. I don't want her reading about the murder or dodging calls or text from Troy or reporters." Goldie answered. "Aren't the cops gonna need to talk to her, though?" Renee asked. "If they leave a message, then we'll call them back, but only the cops." She answered. "And you guys don't need to speak to anybody either. If they have questions tell them to talk to Troy or to leave a message." They nodded their understanding. "Okay now you go home. You still have your keys, right? Make sure you check on the place from time to time, but no parties!" she said. "No parties." they said in unison. "What about the rent and Con Edison?" Renee asked. "They're set up on autopay." Goldie answered. They kissed her goodbye and made her promise to call as soon as she could. Goldie had to close the door quickly, but before they saw her tears. She honestly didn't know if she'd ever see them again and it was breaking her heart, but this was what needed to be done.

Goldie had first suspected something was off with Misty when she heard the twins talking about the weird books she was reading. They were about murder and drugs. As far as she knew, Misty had never been interested in either of those things. She knew she had been seeing a new guy and just wanted to make sure that he wasn't taking her down this new path. Misty wasn't a follower, but Goldie knew firsthand how much damage could be done by trusting the wrong person. So, she did a little snooping and found the books and the notes Misty put in them. Then she found the wigs and clothing she'd used to disguise herself. She wasn't sure what to make of it. She'd hoped that Misty was researching ideas for a new show. Her hopes were shattered when she read the article about Paul's death. The article said that his body had been found in his apartment after about a week. The article was a few weeks old by the time Goldie read it, and it seemed to be right around the time that she had met Troy. When Misty told her about the attack, she told her the names of the boys that did it. Goldie did some digging, much like Misty did, and found them all online. Over the years, she googled the names to see if they had ever done anything like that again. So, when she saw Paul's name, she knew exactly who he was, and she had a pretty good idea of who'd killed him. After the story of Kevin's death came out, she still wasn't sure until she saw Misty's face one night when they were watching the news and the story came on. At first, she looked afraid. Then relieved when even they didn't recognize her in the video. Then pure satisfaction. Anyone else would have missed it, but Goldie knew her daughter. She laid awake a few nights and worried, but she could clearly take care of herself. And if anyone deserved revenge, it was Misty. Goldie envied her. She was so strong. Life had done it's best to knock her down and keep her there, but she wouldn't stay down. And when she got up, she was even stronger than before. Goldie packed their bags. She grabbed things she thought Misty would want. To prepare for this day, Goldie had acquired fake IDs for herself and Misty, purchased a car using her new identity and withdrawn enough cash to last them for a few months. She went downstairs to load up the car and stopped to look around. She snapped a few pictures with her prepaid phone so that she could look at them when she got homesick. She was going to miss this place, but she couldn't stay without Misty. A few trips later, she was done. "This would have been faster if the twins were here." She said to herself. But they would have had too many questions about the car. She looked around the apartment one last time and cried. She allowed herself to shed those tears because they were well deserved. She'd spent most of her life here. Maybe she would be back. "You never know where the day may take you!" She said to the empty apartment. She did one last walk through and left.

Troy was at his desk watching the video of the delivery person entering and exiting Ryan's building. His captain had kept his word and given him access to the evidence, hoping he'd see something they didn't. He'd spoken to Ryan's family again and notified the team. He assured them he wouldn't rest until the person responsible was caught. He hadn't told them about the serial killer angle because he didn't have any proof that it was related. Even though he knew it was. He leaned back in his chair and his pen rolled off the desk. He bent down to pick it up and something in the video caught his eye. Her shoes looked familiar. He enlarged the image. "Oh yeah, Misty has those." He said to the screen. He remembered when she wore them. She was so happy because they were a limited edition, and she'd gotten the last pair in her size. He did a quick search and found out how many were sold. Only 500. So, Misty and the killer had the same limited edition Nikes? Did she have hers on that night? He tried to remember, but he couldn't. He was so focused on her and Ryan's injuries that night. His mind started racing. Could she be her? Why would she be her? Why would she? He said as he stood up. "No! No, no, no, no!" He shouted. "You okay? What's up?" An officer asked. "Yeah, yeah!" Troy answered. "I missed something." He sat down and stared at the image. He had to talk to Misty. He had to see her shoes before he told his captain or any of the detectives. He had to be positive before he opened that can of worms. He knew Misty. He loved Misty. She couldn't be her. He grabbed his things and headed to the hospital.

Goldie arrived at the hospital just before the morning visiting hours were over. When she walked into the room, Misty was writing something on a notepad. "I hope that's not a goodbye letter for me." Goldie said. Her voice startled Misty. "Huh? No, no." Misty replied. "I was just." She stopped. "How did you know?" She asked. Goldie said, "A mother knows." She closed the door behind her. "Now get dressed." She said, handing Misty a bag. Misty stared at Goldie and then at the bag. "What's going on?" She asked. "We are leaving! Get dressed!" Goldie said, pulling items from the bag. Misty was confused, but she got up and got dressed. Before they left, she took one of the letters she'd written and placed it on the bed. Troy was written on the envelope. She had been planning her escape, but she wanted to say goodbye to Goldie, the twins, and Troy. She'd asked one of the nurses to bring her pen and paper and four envelopes. The only letter she'd finished was Troy's. She explained everything by telling him her story from the beginning. She asked him not to blame himself for not seeing it. "This is how it had to end." She said as she placed the envelope on the pillow. When they left the hospital Misty followed Goldie to a parking lot a few blocks away. When Goldie opened the car door, Misty stopped and said, "Who's car is this?" "Ours!" Goldie answered. "When did we get a car? How long was I in the hospital? Did I go into a coma or something?" Misty was rattling off question after question. Goldie burst into laughter. "No, you did not slip into a coma. I'll explain everything. Can we go now?" She asked, opening the door for Misty. "If we're leaving town, I gotta make a stop first." Misty said. Goldie gave her an exasperated look. "It'll be quick. 30 minutes tops." "Okay where to?" Goldie asked. "Banco Popular." Misty said. Goldie gave her an approving look and asked, "safe deposit box?" Misty said, "yeah." Goldie backhanded Misty's breast and said, "That's my girl!"

As they drove off, Troy was arriving at the hospital. When he got to Misty's room, he thought she'd gone for a walk or for testing. He was waiting for her to come back when the nurse came in to check on her." Do you know when she'll be back?" He asked. "I don't know where she's gone." The nurse answered. "She's not scheduled for any test right now. I was coming to check her vitals." "Could she be walking around somewhere?" He asked. "It's possible. Let me see if anyone has seen her." The nurse said, as she walked out of the room. Troy walked over to the bed and saw the envelope with his name on it. "No, come on. Don't do this to me Misty." He said to the empty room. He picked up the envelope and left before the nurse got back. When he got home, he sat down and read Misty's letter. "I know you want to come after me she wrote, but don't. I'm not evil. I'm just trying to right a wrong." She told him about the night of the attack. She told him how Ryan had raped and beat her along with the others. She told him she hoped he hadn't known about that part because if he did and he was still friends with Ryan, he wasn't the man she thought he was. She told him how she left the hospital and went to the city and met Goldie. About getting her new face and discovering her skill for designing costumes, all while plotting her revenge. She got to the night they'd met, and that she'd killed Paul that night. He closed his eyes and tried to replay that night. What did he miss? "Nothing." he said. There wasn't anything to miss. He knew he'd be asked these questions over and over as soon as he told his captain. "Do you have to tell him?" A voice in his head asked. "I'm a cop!" He replied. "I planned this for so long and then I met you. I almost gave up the whole thing to be with you, but then you brought Ryan to me, and I knew that was a sign to continue my mission." He read the rest of the letter. She apologized for hurting him. She ended it with, "I will always love you!" He sat in his chair and cried.

When Misty came out of the bank, she was carrying a large duffel bag. "We have matching luggage I see." Goldie said and lifted the back seat. There was another duffel in a hidden compartment. Misty laughed and placed her bag next to it. Before Goldie pulled out of the parking spot, Misty asked, "Are you sure you want to do this? I have to leave but this is your home." Goldie looked at Misty and said Baby, you're my daughter and I love you! You are my home!"

Author's Note

Misty's story popped up in my head a long time ago, but I didn't have the courage to start writing. I always thought I needed help because I hadn't had any formal training. I believe that a good book should transport you to the world that the writer created, and I didn't think I could do that. I asked my sister Shavahn, for help, and she gave me the best advice ever. "Just start." She said "Then if you need help, we'll help you." So, I did just that and here we are. So, for anyone waiting for the right time to start a new journey, here it is. Just start and see where the road takes you!